The Comeback

Erica Frost

Published by Erica Frost, 2023.

THE COMEBACK

First edition. September 29, 2023.

Copyright © 2023 Erica Frost.

ISBN: 979-8223396673

Written by Erica Frost.

Table of Contents

The Comeback
College Second Chance Romance

By: Erica Frost

Foreword

An ex is an ex for a reason. But what about second chances?

College starts off well. New place. New people. New love. Then, the love disappears, and I'm left alone in a new place with new people. I feel like a child lost in an adult world, and I don't know where to turn.

Just when things are slowly settling in, I see him. The bad boy who broke my heart. Football is all he does now. Football and all those girls that surround him all the time. We meet at a party, and it's the most awkward meeting ever.

Something is telling me to give him a second chance, but I'm scared. How could two strangers, enemies almost, become lovers again?

The Comeback

Chapter One

E lsie

"Do you really think I want to spend the evening watching drunken jocks hit on the Cappa Beta girls?" I roll my eyes at my roommate Rachel, grateful not to be one of them.

We all know the type. Pretty little airheads. Perfect hair. Perfect teeth. Perfect everything. As opposed to the rest of us, mortal girls, who have to deal with bad hair days, braces and of course, clever comments which we might be forced to dumb down in order for the guys not to feel threatened by a clever girl.

"You could spend the evening being hit on by those same drunken jocks," Rachel tells me, giving me a suggestion which, coming from her, sounds very weird. In fact, coming from anyone, it would come off as weird because that is about the last thing I would want to have done to me.

I find this weird because she's usually the voice of reason. Not only that, but she is also my roommate, my best friend, and pretty much my Jiminy Cricket, who is now telling Pinocchio to actually go out and have fun. What the heck? Has the world gone topsy turvy without me noticing it?

"I think I'll pass," I tell her indifferently, shrugging.

She walks up to me, locking her arm with mine. Her long, raven black hair is the first thing that catches everyone's attention. Then, it's her striking green eyes. She's like a wicked fairy from some old, forgotten Andersen fairy tale. Only, she's not wicked. At least, not all the time and not to me. That's what counts. Having a best friend who would kick someone's ass for you and look flawless while doing it.

"I think you need to get laid," she tells me, matter-of-factly, as if one night of mindless sex will solve all the problems I've been having lately.

"If only the solution was that simple," I pretend to sigh. To be quite honest, I think her suggestion would only make an already complicated situation even more complicated, but I don't say this out loud.

"You're the one making it difficult," she tells me. She might have a point here, but once again, I don't say it out loud. I don't want to give her the satisfaction.

"In any case, I really don't feel like going," I admit, whining a little, hoping she'll leave me alone.

She tilts her head to the side and gives me an introspective glance. "You're not gonna make me play the favor card, are you?"

My eyes widen in disbelief. "Come on," I frown. "Not for this."

"No, no, no," she shakes her head at me, showing me number three with her fingers. "I got three favors. Count them. Three favors which we agreed I can claim at any time, night or day. I'm claiming one now."

"Seriously?" I blurt out. "For this stupid party?"

"Yes, seriously," she confirms. "Now, go and get dressed, before I use another favor and make you wear a mini skirt that shows half your ass."

Luckily, she didn't make good on that threat, and I end up wearing just a pair of jeans with a cute little, cropped top. When I check myself in the mirror, I have to admit I don't look half bad. I washed my hair just this morning, so it's flowing down my back. I consider a ponytail, but eventually, just leave it as it is. A bit of mascara, some gloss and I'm good to go.

When I appear before Rachel, she eyes me top to bottom.

"Tight jeans showing off your butt? OK. Showing some skin there as well? Better than OK. You look good enough to eat, girl," she winks at me, and I can't help but chuckle. Somehow, she manages to make even the crappiest days better. It's a skill, really and not everyone has it. I sure don't.

We head to the party, and by the time we reach the Omega Lambda frat house, the party is already in full swing. The music is blasting loudly. A small group of guys is chugging beer on the front porch, while girls are cheering them on.

I turn to Rachel, with one raised eyebrow.

"Don't judge a book by its cover, smartass," she tells me as she pulls me inside.

"This is not a book," I murmur. "This is a comic."

She looks at me, then we both chuckle out loud, as we make our way through the crowd of people who are dancing, talking, kissing and groping each other. We reach the refreshments table, and Rachel grabs us two still unopened cans of beer.

"Just one," I say, accepting it. "Then, your favor has been paid off."

"Five drinks or three hours," she tells me with a shrug.

"Who came up with that rule?" I laugh.

"I did," she tells me. "Just now."

"I can't do either," I admit.

"Three hours isn't much," she says.

"Around these people?"

I turn around. I doubt I know anyone here. And I don't care to get to know them. I make a disgruntled face, as we head to the other room. The music is even louder there, but Rachel doesn't seem to mind. She immediately finds an object of interest, in the form of a tall, dark and handsome stranger, who immediately returns her gaze. I know she just wants my permission to leave, so I let her go.

"Are you sure?" she asks.

"I'll be fine," I nod. "If you don't see me, that means I've had enough and went home."

"No," she shakes her head. "You can't. Besides, I'm just going to chat him up a bit. He might not be interested in me."

I chuckle at that. "Has that ever happened?"

She shrugs as she walks backwards, grinning. The moment she starts talking to that guy, I can see he's already eating out of the palm of her hand. I sigh to myself. She makes it seem so easy. And I'm sure that it is for her. But for girls like me, there's nothing more difficult. I had that one boyfriend in first year, and everything after that seemed to be a flop.

A new song blasts off and I feel like my ears will start bleeding if I stay here. I glance at Rachel, waiting for her to look back at me. When she does, I mouth the word outside, and point to the door. She nods and gestures a little with her fingers. I nod, giving her a thumbs up, then I head out.

Once again, another flop. Honestly, I don't know what it is I was even expecting to find here, surely not someone normal you can have a proper conversation with. When I find my way out, I realize that it's just as crowded on the front porch. The same guys are chugging even more beer. The same girls are cheering them on.

Then, I notice a small passage around the house. I figure maybe there's less people behind there. Maybe I could take a breather before heading back in and convincing Rachel that there's no point in staying here.

I walk around the house, noticing several trees and a manicured lawn. And just as I turn around the nearest tree, I notice a guy standing, with his pants down half his butt, as he's peeing against the tree.

I quickly jump backward, turning around, and frowning.

"Oh, come on!" I shout at him. "Were you born in a barn?"

He doesn't say anything at first. I hear the sound of the zipper being pulled up, then he takes a few steps.

"All the bathrooms inside were taken," he tells me.

Immediately upon hearing his voice, I realize I know him from somewhere. Somewhere very private, very personal. Somewhere like my own heart, my own bed.

Of all the people to meet...

I turn around, and there he is. Callum Holland. The reason why the entire first year of college was so wonderful, and every other day after that was such a hell. But not for him. When we met, he was a scrawny thing, and now, he looks like a boulder that got separated from a mountain. I guess that's not a bad thing at all when you're the star quarterback. Still, I preferred how he used to be. Not that I'd be given the chance to choose anyway, nor would I want to.

"Elsie," he recognizes me immediately. At least that. "What..." he starts but doesn't continue.

"What am I doing here?" I continue his thought. "Honestly, I have no idea myself."

I can't take my eyes off him. He looks even better than he did back when we were dating. He was just a scrawny little guy, and now, he's twice the size he was back then. Even his facial structure changed somehow, giving him a rough edgy look. No wonder all the girls are dying to sleep with him.

"I just went out for some fresh air, only to find you pissing against a tree," I frown, wanting to make him as uncomfortable as I was feeling now. But one look at him assures me he already feels uncomfortable enough. After all, he was the one being caught with half his butt out.

"I told you," he repeats. "No– "

"... free toilets," I cut him off, finishing his thought again. "Got it. Still doesn't make it nice."

"How have you been?" He asks, obviously desperate to change the topic.

A part of me wants to tell him the truth. The whole unadulterated truth of how miserable I've been, of how I even started to doubt my choice of profession and now I have no freakin' idea what I am doing here. All those things are on the tip of my tongue, dying to spill. But I manage to keep them subdued.

"I'm fine," I give him the proverbial reply which in other words usually means, it's none of your fucking business how I'm doing. Then, I ask him the same, although I couldn't care less. "You?"

"Fine," he replies, nodding. "Have you–" he starts, but isn't allowed to finish, because a girl jumps from somewhere in the bushes and grabs him by the arm, pulling him back to the house.

"Come, Cal," she purrs into his ear. She is obviously drunk. He seems a bit, too. I guess I'm the only sober one here in this entire place. And that's why I feel so out of place.

"Sorry, Elsie," he tells me, fighting to stay here, but the tugging on his arm is getting more and more demanding.

"Go, Cal," I repeat his nickname, which has obviously become what they call him now. Before, he was always Callum. He always loved his name and didn't like it being shortened. But I guess things change. People change. It's just how life is.

He seems as if he wants to say something else, but then changes his mind at the last minute. "Nice seeing you," he tells me, then disappears into the darkness.

"Yeah," I frown, taking a sip of the beer in my hand. What a flop.

I go back inside and find Rachel, who's examining the guy's tonsils with her tongue. I pat her on the shoulder, and neither of them seems particularly pleased I did that.

"I'm gonna go back," I shout against the music.

"Not even an hour," she shouts back. "And not even one beer."

"I had more than enough excitement for one night," I say, putting my beer down on a nearby table, signaling that I'm really done. "You can stay if you want."

She immediately jumps from the guy's lap. "We came together, we go back together. You know the rules." I smile at her words.

The guy pulls her by the hand. "Stay, gorgeous," he urges. "Let her go on her own. She'll be fine."

Rachel frowns at him. "That's not what good friends do."

With those words, she locks her arm with mine, and we head outside, into the fresh air. Sure, some nights are total flops, but it's all worth it when you're going back with the same person you came with. Your best friend.

Chapter Two

Callum

I wake up around noon. Maybe even later. My head feels like a boxing bag that's been hit all night long, over and over again. I definitely shouldn't have overdone it with the beers. A beer hangover isn't bad, but it lasts a whole day, no matter what you do.

I realize that I fell asleep in one of the rooms of the frat house. I was too wasted to drive back to the apartment I'm renting, just outside of college campus. On one side, it's nice being away from it all every night, but at the same time, you want to stay here, where all the happenings are. The good thing is that the frat house doors are always open if I want to crash the night.

In fact, many doors opened for me in the last three years, ever since I became a star quarterback, doors I never even knew existed. People treat you differently. They say your name differently. They address you differently. I guess I should have expected that. And I liked it. I still do. I mean, what's there not to like?

Everyone is smiling at you, patting you on the back. You can't seem to do wrong. And I have to admit, the feeling is good. Hell, it's more than good. I finally feel like I'm living the life I always wanted.

At that moment, the door barges open, and Shawn, a surfer-looking guy with a tanned face and dark honey colored hair which is falling in whips down to his shoulders grins upon seeing me.

"Yo, Cal," he tells me. "Did you hit that fine looking thing last night?"

I frown, looking to my side. There's no one else there. "Obviously not," I reply, not wanting to reveal that I don't really remember who he's referring to as that fine looking thing. There were so many nameless girls, all pretty, all willing. It's difficult to pinpoint one when they all seem so much alike, both physically and in the way they think.

That's the part that sometimes gets me thinking. They all always agree with you, no matter what you say, no matter how stupid your statement is. At first, it was interesting. Funny, even. It's still fun, but sometimes, you just miss a good old proper conversation. Not that I'd ever tell Shawn that, or any of the other guys. They seem perfectly at ease with the situation. They wouldn't change a thing. If I say I would, then they'd start looking at me differently. So, it's best just to be quiet and not make too many waves. After all, things are going great. Why spoil that?

Then suddenly, I return to the present moment, and it hits me. I saw Elsie last night. Actually, I didn't see her. She saw me. Pissing against a tree?

"Fuck," I murmur to myself, covering my face with my palm.

"Did you?" Shawn thinks I'm talking to him. "Fuck her?"

"No," I frown, getting up from the bed, and feeling the leftover nausea and dizziness take over. Not one of my finest moments, I have to admit that.

"The beer still hasn't left your body, huh?" Shawn asks. "We got some alcohol-free Bloody Marys down in the kitchen. Want me to fetch you one?"

"Sure," I sigh, nodding.

I sit on the edge of the bed, feeling somewhat better, but that's only because I'm not moving, and my eyes are focused on one spot on the wall. If I start walking, I might drop down to the ground. So, I don't risk it.

I watch Shawn get out of the room, leaving me alone with my jumbled thoughts. I saw Elsie last night. This thought keeps swarming inside my mind, and I have no idea what to do with it. I wondered occasionally what it would be like when we stumbled onto each other like this, somewhere unexpectedly, but that never happened. I guess we just didn't hang out with the same people. Until last night, that is.

Our story always felt somehow... unfinished. I was the one who ended things, feeling that in order to succeed as a professional athlete, I needed to focus on my career and studies, which would eventually get me there. I couldn't allow myself distractions. I didn't tell her this in such a blunt way, of course. I just said something along the lines of we're drifting apart, it's not you it's me. That sort of bullshit. But I should have known that she's too smart for such stupid lines. Only by the time I said it, it was too late to fix it and be honest with her.

I look around myself, realizing that I haven't really done well in that respect. I've been surrounded by different kinds of distractions all this time. There have been constant parties, almost every night, and as the star quarterback, I have to attend them. And that's not the worst part. Attending is fine, but you have to drink. Not just one or two beers, but you gotta chug until you pass out. That was the worst part. The only time I was exempt from this was before a game. And we're not taking a break, so I can't use that as an excuse, because everyone knows it when we're lining up.

I think I haven't even realized up to this point that she wasn't a distraction. I have made her into one, in my own mind. And seeing her last night, reminded me of the asshole that I was to her, when breaking up. I could have done it in a better way. She deserved so much better.

I have no idea why these thoughts are inside of me now. It's probably the fact that I saw her while drunk, and my mind brought back all the memories of the good times we had together. Because the good times were really good.

Again, I look around, at what I traded for her. It was worth it. I'm sure it was.

Shawn immediately returns with a tall glass of something red, which I'm guessing is the Bloody Mary he mentioned. He hands it to me, then chuckles when he notices I'm eyeing it with suspicion. I have absolutely no appetite for anything. My stomach rumbles at the very thought of taking in anything other than water.

"It's alcohol free, I swear," he assures me, with a grin. "The coach will need you totally clean for the game the day after tomorrow, you know that."

I nod. "Honestly, I don't feel all that swell right now."

"It's nothing a shower can't fix," Shawn tells me.

I usually don't overdo it with the beer or drinks in general. But we were celebrating our latest football victory, and as the one mostly responsible for that, I had to accept a toast from everyone who raised their glass to me. And there were a lot of people doing that.

I remember that Madison was there as well, following me around. It also hits me then that she was the one who dragged me away from Elsie, back inside. She usually seized every chance to get me to go to bed with her, and I'm wondering how come she's not here. Something must have made her change her plans. Because I was drunk enough to do it.

Sober, I'd think twice. We already slept together several times, and even though I told her I'm not looking for anything serious, she keeps hoping that if she stays around and keeps herself available to me, I'll somehow change my mind. That's not how these things work. Honestly, I'm not all that sure how they work, but it's not like this.

The past year has been a vague swirl of nameless girls. A part of me doesn't like the man I've turned into, but it's a little voice deep down, which I manage to drown easily. Especially when I've got booze around or my other team members. They help me focus on something else, something that matters, and that is success.

"Need a ride back to your place?" Shawn suggests, bringing me back to the present moment. This aftermath of my drunken night is making me rethink all my life decisions, it seems. And it doesn't feel very good.

"I won't say no," I grin, glancing at the glass in my hand. I'm still considering it, although I should just down it, without thinking. That would be the most painless way to go. Then, if my stomach rebels against it, well... I'll cross that bridge when I get to it.

"But not before you chug that down, like you were chugging beer down last night," he chuckles.

"Don't remind me," I shake my head, feeling that nausea come back again at the very thought of putting something in my stomach, let alone actually doing it. But I know I'll have to. It really is a good cure, cancels out the acidity or whatever. The point is that it works.

So, I close my eyes, and take three big gulps, emptying the entire glass. My stomach protests violently. But I take it all down. I swallow heavily, feeling the leftover taste wreak havoc inside my mouth. But mercifully, a few moments later, the taste disappears. My stomach calms down a little. Maybe this day won't be so bad, after all.

"Better?" he asks.

I shrug.

"It should be," he adds. "Give it time." He gets up and walks over to the door. "I'll just go grab my car keys and I'm waiting for you outside."

A moment later, and I'm alone again in the room. I get up, still dizzy, but I manage to put the rest of my clothes on and find my way out. The house seems empty, mostly because the guys are still sleeping in their rooms. I wonder why Shawn's up, but I'm not questioning it further. I have a ride home.

He drops me off and it's just like he said. A shower does me good. It brings me back. It refreshes both my mind and my body, and I can finally think straight. Even my stomach has managed to calm down, as I slump onto my sofa, and turn on the TV. I watch mindlessly, as The Godfather allows some guy to kiss his ring finger, in exchange for a favor. But I can barely focus on the story.

I'm still thinking about Elsie. I know I shouldn't. Our story is done. At least, I thought it was done, until I saw her last night. I don't remember her being that beautiful. And I was like the last loser in the world, pissing against a tree.

Fucking hell.

Chapter Three

Elsie

I know it's time to wake up, but I don't want to. At this point, the blissful state of sleep is so much more preferable to my waking life. I don't open my eyes, but my mind is awake, and that is enough to remember that I'm nowhere where I thought I would be at this point.

"Wakey, wakey," I hear Rachel say, trying to pull on my cover from my feet.

"No," I whine, pulling the covers back up and over my head. "I'm not getting up today at all."

Rachel laughs melodiously, letting go. "You think that'll work?" she asks me.

"I dunno," I reply in a muffled tone. "But I can try."

"Come on," she urges. "I'll get us a coffee from the machine, and we can enjoy the morning."

"We could enjoy the morning," Rachel corrects me, "if you would get up, get dressed and I could treat you to a coffee at the Starbucks."

There's only one Starbucks on campus, and it's usually crowded, especially on a Sunday morning. As if people don't have anything better to do than drink Starbucks coffee the moment they open their eyes.

Then, I realize I'm one of those people. I want a Starbucks coffee the moment I open my eyes. But I said I'm not getting out of bed.

"Any chance you could get us both a coffee and bring it back here?" I ask, already knowing what her reply will be.

Rachel chuckles, and I feel the thump of something soft that has fallen right on my head. She threw a pillow at me.

"No way, Jose," she tells me. "I'm only offering the muddy water from down the hall to be brought to you, your majesty. If you want a proper coffee, you'll have to walk there with me to get it."

I pull down the cover only up to my nose, and I pretend to glare at her.

"You are a meanie," I hiss playfully, and we both chuckle.

"Come on," she repeats. "It's a lovely day. Sunny and all that shit. Let's go for a walk."

I think about it for a moment. Sure, I could stay here and feel sorry for myself, or I could go out and focus on something else. That is always easy to do with Rachel. She's full of funny stories, and great at making you feel better when you're down.

That's one of the reasons I like her so much. At first, I thought that her overly bubbly and direct nature wouldn't be my thing, but I was wrong. She's so easy to like. I wish I had at least half of her likeability. But I guess it's the way she charms others, while making it seem so effortless. That, plus she doesn't give a rat's ass what others think about her. That has always been the most difficult part for me. I do care what others think. I've always cared, and I think I've cared too much. That is one of the most difficult lessons I have yet to learn.

"You made up your mind already?" I hear her ask.

I pull down the cover from my face, and the heavy light oozing from the window hits my eyes mercilessly. I immediately hide back underneath the covers.

"Are you a vampire?" she chuckles at me.

"Almost," I mumble.

Then, I slowly adjust my eyes to the light, only to sit down on the bed. I still feel caught in that state between sleep and fully being awake. A few moments, and I'm completely awake.

"Wear something cute," she urges me, as she opens my wardrobe, and starts going through my dresses and t-shirts.

"Why?" I frown.

"Because you never know who's gonna be checking you out," she turns to me, winking mischievously.

I can't resist laughing. "That is the last thing on my mind right now."

"I know," she sighs heavily, as if she's carrying the burden of the world. "I honestly don't know what to do with you."

"Nothing?" I shrug.

"No," she shakes her head, extracting a cute little flowery dress from my closet. "I feel personally responsible for you. When you don't get laid, it actually pains me."

"Pains you?" I chuckle again. "You're weird."

"No, you're weird," she corrects me with a smile, as she brings me the dress. "Here. Wear this."

"But that's my dress for going out."

"You are going out," she says squinting at me. "For a coffee. Doesn't that count as going out?"

"I guess so." Now it's my turn to sigh, because this morning is obviously going to follow a plan that Rachel has already come up with in her mind.

"You're too young to be so indifferent to life, Elsie," she tells me softly, sitting down on the bed next to me.

"I'm not indifferent," I say, realizing that our current conversation consists of trying to prove the other one wrong. "I just... don't care."

Once again, we both chuckle out loud.

"OK, Mrs. Nietzsche," she makes fun of me. "Get dressed and let's go pour some wake-up liquid in you. Maybe you'll be in a better mood then."

As always, Rachel is right. I get ready as quickly as I can, and the moment we head outside, I feel better. The campus is not as busy as usual, because half of the people have decided to sleep in. The other half can probably be found at Starbucks. But we won't be staying there anyway. We usually pick up our coffee and head over to the small fountain, with a circular set of benches, that warm up nicely in the sun, and when you sit on them, you feel like a tender hug enveloped you whole.

We grab our coffees, then head to the fountain, as we usually do. The sound of the water feels calming, and every once in a while, you hear the flutter of pigeons' wings, as they get spooked by a passerby, flying high up into the air.

"I take it you didn't have much fun last night," Rachel asks, taking a sip of her coffee. The name on hers reads Rach. Even to strangers, she is Rach.

"Not really," I admit with a sigh, staring somewhere into the distance.

"Should I ask what it was you didn't like, or maybe the list of things you did like is shorter?" She tries a joke, and I smile.

"I saw Callum," I say it out loud, realizing that this has been the sentence I've been dying to say since I woke up.

Last night, when we got back home, I was still under the influence of seeing him. Even if I did share this little tidbit with her, I wouldn't know how to comment on it. So, I figured I'd sleep on it, and then share it with her, with a clearer mind. Only, my mind doesn't feel much clearer. In fact, it feels even more muddy than last night. I hate it when that happens.

"You did?" she asks. "I guess that was bound to happen."

"Mhm," I nod.

"Did you speak with him?"

"A little," I nod again. "Saw him pissing against a tree behind the house."

"You... what?" Rachel's eyes widen in shock, then she bursts out into boisterous laughter. A few passersby turn around to see what the commotion is all about, but she doesn't care. It takes her a few moments to calm down, but she's still smiling. "So, you caught him with his pants down, but not in a good way."

"You could say that, yes," I chuckle, because that was the same thing I thought to myself when I saw him. Great minds think alike, even when they think about nonsense.

"Was he still as good as before?" she winks at me.

"What? No!" I frown, pretending to be disgusted, which I was, at least a little. "I didn't look. Come on..."

"You can keep saying that to yourself, but we all know we'd look," she shrugs, still teasing me. "Although, you know what he's working with from before."

"I'm not discussing this," I shake my head, unable to suppress a chuckle.

"Suit yourself," she says, taking another sip of her coffee. "But I think this was fate."

"Fate?"

"Yes," she assures me, staring at the fountain. I look in the same direction, enjoying the sparkle of the sun on the watery surface. There is definitely the promise of a lovely day, and I wonder whether we can seize it somehow, without just staying in our rooms for the rest of the afternoon. It seems like such a waste.

Then, she turns to me, and stares me dead in the face. "It's a sign." She says it so seriously, almost like an old fortune teller, who will tell you that you're about to die unless you leave a good tip. And she'll make you believe it, too.

"A sign of what, you smartass?" I ask, actually enjoying this nonsensical conversation.

"A sign that you, my dear friend, need to get laid."

Once again, she says it so gravely that I burst out into laughter, just like she did a moment ago, and I can't stop. When I finally do, I realize she's still serious.

"Thanks for being worried about my sexual health, but I'm fine," I joke.

"I'm really worried," she lowers her voice. "You haven't gotten laid in what... months?"

"Uhm, well..." I push a loose strand of hair behind my ear a little nervously.

"Oh my God... don't tell me it's been years." Her eyes widen in disbelief.

I shrug. "I haven't really slept with anyone since Callum."

"No one?" she asks, incredulous.

"Nope," I shake my head.

"Not even Dustin?" She mentions the guy I went on two dates with, but I realized that it wouldn't work. There was nothing wrong with him, I just wasn't feeling the spark, so when he asked me out on a third date, I said I wasn't interested. I guess I haven't really updated Rachel on that development, since she was home during that time.

"Nope," I repeat. "No one."

"Oh, you poor, poor thing," she says, taking my hand into hers, and patting it sympathetically.

"I'm fine, Rach," I chuckle. "You make it sound like I'm terminally ill or something."

"Do you know girls can get blue balls as well?"

"What?" I roll my eyes, unable to suppress another bout of laughter. "You're insane, do you know that?"

"Na-ha, I'm serious," she continues on the low down, as if we're in on a conspiracy, and we mustn't get overheard.

"I don't even wanna know what that looks like," I reply.

"You already know," she whispers, leaning closer to me. "You don't even know you know."

This time, we both giggle, almost like schoolgirls, and somehow, she makes it all better with her blue balls talk and signs and fates. For all the heartache college years have brought me, there is one thing I will never regret, and that is meeting Rachel. She enriches my life in so many ways, and yet, if I began to tell her any of this, she would just brush it off, because that's how she is. She doesn't want you to make anything about her. It's always about you. She is there for you, there to make you feel better, and on days such as this one, I appreciate it more than ever.

"Good coffee, huh?" I ask, trying to change the topic, but she lifts one eyebrow at me.

"It won't work, you know," she says. "I really think you should reevaluate the fact that you haven't seen Callum in so long, and now, out of the blue, you stumble upon him. That has to mean something."

"No, it doesn't," I shrug. "We go to the same college. Meeting or not meeting each other is just a matter of coincidence."

This makes sense. I know it does. Discussing otherwise would just raise hopes that I managed to keep under control all this time. The last thing I want now is letting those hopes run free.

We finish our coffee and head back to the room, trying to come up with a little trip off campus grounds, to enjoy the day.

Chapter Four

Callum

It's the last class for the day, and I'm looking forward to some downtime once it ends, and before practice starts early in the evening. The weekend was fun, but now it's time to get down to serious business.

I wave to Shawn and a few other guys, heading in the opposite direction. Things are better when you have stuff to do, then you don't have so much to think about. Thinking is dangerous. It makes you wonder about all those passed up opportunities and chances you turned your back to and then–

"Hey, you!" Someone's voice pulls me back to the present moment. "Always lost in thought."

I lift my gaze and realize it's Madison. "Hey, Maddie." I smile at her, trying to just pass her by, but I know she won't allow that. So, I stop.

Her heavy perfume hits my nostrils forcefully. Then again, everything she does is forceful. I can't imagine why her perfume would be any different.

"I had a nice time at the party," she purrs into my ear, leaning closer to me.

I try to remember if we did anything. I think I'd remember. We didn't have sex, that's for sure. But did we make out? Possibly, if she got hold of me when I was most drunk. The last thing I remember was her pulling me away from Elsie, back into the house. God knows what happened.

Exactly because I can't remember, I can't let this happen again. This is not who I am.

"Yeah, me, too," I tell her, not really sure what else there is to say.

"I was thinking, maybe we could get together tonight and... you know, study," she tells me, licking her upper lip as she's smiling seductively.

I look at her. She's every man's dream. Her long dark hair, her chestnut eyes, those full lips and a body to die for. She can even be far less annoying than she usually is, when she wants to. And yet, there's nothing about her that attracts me in a way a woman should attract a man long-term.

I know what the guys would say. So what? Just keep banging her while the banging is good. I can hear those words as plain as daylight. And once again, I remind myself that it's not who I am. It's not who I was before. But somehow, I have reached this place in life. Everything I've done has led me up to this point in time and place, and while some things are what I expected they would be, other things are completely the opposite.

"Yeah, I don't think I'll have the time for that," I tell her, hoping that she will get the hint.

"How about tomorrow night then?" she asks again.

She's not taking her eyes off me, with those long eyelashes. She's wearing a tight, low-cut t-shirt, and she knows how low that cut is. She has to. Her jeans are so tight you'd have to peel them off her, because there's no other way they are coming off her. But I have no desire to take any part of her clothes off. I've done it once. Actually, more than once, and that was it. I made it perfectly clear that I wasn't looking for anything serious and I thought we agreed on that. Now, it turns out I was the only one who was in agreement, because she kept pushing for more every time she saw me. And it was becoming too much.

"Listen, Maddie," I tell her, scratching the back of my neck a little nervously.

I have to tell her I don't want her. And that is not something anyone wants to hear. I have to make sure to say it right this time, and not be the jackass I was to Elsie. The truth is always the right way to go, even though it might seem like it's too much to handle. Maddie is a big girl. She'll be fine.

"Yes?" she chirps at me, batting those long eyelashes expectantly.

I inhale deeply, then continue. "You're a... great girl, you really are. But I'm really not looking to date right now."

"You think that," she corrects me, patting me on the nose with her index finger. "But you have no idea how swell it is to be dating me."

Of course, she's not taking me seriously. I doubt there's ever been someone who refused her advances. She thinks I'm joking. But I'm not.

"I'm sure it is," I smile. "Only... I don't want to date anyone. I have so much to focus on, my studies, the practice. I... I just can't give a girl the attention she needs."

I'm still trying to be the good guy here and tell her nicely no. But I guess when you tell someone no nicely, they always think they can talk you into changing your mind.

"I'm sure you have no problems in that department," she continues to purr seductively into my ear, stepping closer and closer to me.

I know what she's doing. She's teasing me, trying to see if she has any effect on me. It works with almost every guy, I'm sure. Who in their right mind would tell her no?

Me.

Why?

I have no fucking idea why. I feel like that party from a few nights ago left me wondering about much more than just my binge drinking. Maybe seeing Elsie brought back some long-forgotten memories, which are now surfacing whether I want them to or not. Strangely, Elsie is the only girl in my mind right now, and not as someone I want to fuck, but actually as someone I want to sit down and have a coffee with. Maybe even try to explain myself to. I feel like I owe her that much.

"Really, Maddie," I continue, wanting to cut this short but not really knowing how to do it, when I've already shot all my responses to her.

Then, she stands right in front of me, with our noses almost touching. She reaches out for my cheek and caresses it softly. I'm ready to pull away when she tries to kiss me, but she doesn't do that. We're just standing there, probably looking like a pair of weirdos, as she's staring me dead in the face, unwilling to look away.

"You're too good for me to give up," she tells me with a sigh. "It's your fault, really."

I almost chuckle out loud to this, but I manage to suppress the urge.

"I will keep coming after you, no matter what it takes," she says.

I've never had a girl be so direct with me, and a part of me actually admires her for it. She sure has more balls than me.

"If you're not ready now, I understand," she smiles a wicked smile. "But I'm sure you'll be ready soon. And I'll be there, waiting."

She catches me off guard and presses her lips to mine. Before I even have time to react, she's already pulled away, and leaving in the opposite direction. I'm left stunned with what just happened. And now I'm surer than ever that I won't be getting her off my back so quickly.

Someone pats me on the back, and I turn around, still lost in the moment.

"Yo, man," Greg, one of my team members, approaches me, clicking his lips with appetite as he watches Maddie leave. "What I'd give to hit that."

"You can have her," I tell him with a dismissive half-shrug. "I don't have anything to do with her."

"Yeah, don't think I haven't tried," he says regretfully, still staring at her ass, which I think she is swaying just a bit more than usually, because she knows someone is looking. "But apparently, she's just got eyes for you, hot stuff."

I roll my eyes at him. What seems a blessing to him is actually a curse for me.

"You ready for practice tonight?" he asks, as we both head in the opposite direction, and he's finally pulled away from Maddie's ass in the distance.

"You know it," I nod. "Coach has been riding me all week."

"That's because you're the star, hot stuff," he teases, wrapping his arms around my shoulders. "And after we win another game, we're celebrating. You know this, right?"

The thought of getting wasted again makes me sick. My stomach remembers the booze, the alcohol-free Bloody Mary, and it rebels violently against all that. I have to come up with a good excuse if I'm to skip the party.

"Yeah, I'll have to see about that," I say, unsure what reason to give him.

"Are you fucking kidding me?" he asks me, incredulous. I know the other guys will react in the same way when he tells them this, but I've realized that I want less distractions in my life, and parties are the biggest distraction there is. Maybe I could slowly start to withdraw from that lifestyle.

Only I know that this lifestyle goes together with being the star quarterback. Your team wants you to be involved in the victory as well as in the celebration. If I avoid them, they're bound to hold it against me. So, the only way to get what I want is to change nothing. The thought doesn't really appeal to me, but I guess that's what I have to do for the time being.

"You have to be there," he tells me. "Otherwise, it won't be a party."

I smile. "I'll do my best. You know I always do."

"That's my boy," he pats me on the shoulder, and we continue to our next class together, talking about unimportant stuff, which I'm not fully focused on.

My mind is all on the upcoming game. That is the only thing I need to focus on right now. As my coach always says, girls are a distraction. Sometimes, distractions are good. Sometimes, they aren't. It is up to us to pinpoint those times. If we manage to do it successfully, we're off to a good start. But if we welcome distractions into our lives at the worst possible moment, then that path won't lead to success, because we're dissipating energy on something that isn't a priority.

Maddie is definitely a distraction. I allowed her to distract me a few times, but that was all I needed. Now, I can focus on what I need to do. I can focus on success and greatness, which I feel are destined for me. This is my time, and I can't allow anyone to take it away from me.

Chapter Five

Elsie

Maybe Rachel is right... maybe.

I keep rewinding that conversation over and over in my mind, making it difficult to focus on my classes throughout the day. But I somehow manage to do it, still wondering whether Rachel is right. She usually is, and that's what's bugging me the most. She usually knows what's best for me, even when I myself am too blind to see it. Then again, I guess that's the characteristic of a true best friend. They will tell you like it is, whether you want to hear it or not. This time, I don't.

Our conversation revolved around Callum, of course, and my need to... in her words, get laid.

I get it. We all need some fun. We all need to unwind. Sex is a great way to do that. I get all that, but I've never been the one-night stand kind of girl. I wouldn't know what to do. I told her this, and she started chuckling, as usual, telling me that I'm making a big deal out of something that is exactly the opposite. Not a big deal at all.

Maybe she's right.

There, I'm doing it again.

I shake my head at myself, holding a Starbucks latte and sitting on a little bench, in the most solitary part of the campus, just outside a small forest. It's my favorite place here, exactly because not everyone passes through here. They prefer to be seen, heard, so they always go through the central part. In my opinion, this place is for those on the margins of the college society, those who do not like being seen or heard that much, but who still have more than enough to say. We just don't like to shout it out loud from the rooftops.

I take a sip of my coffee, enjoying the sun going down. It's still early in the evening. Rachel has already informed me that she's bringing home some guy. Hank, Frank, something like that. I don't even try to remember their names. I doubt she does as well.

His name is irrelevant. What is relevant, though, is the fact that I can't come back to our room any time soon. That means that I have several hours to kill somewhere. The Starbucks café was full, so that wasn't even an option. I could always go to the library, which is where I figured I'd head, as soon as I finish my coffee. I needed the caffeine boost, because God knows how long I'll have to stay out. She said she'd text me when it's safe to return. Her own words.

When you share a room with someone, you have to make it work somehow. Sharing a room with Rachel is actually very simple and straightforward, because we always meet each other halfway. I know if I had someone to bring to the room, she'd do the same for me.

I sigh at the thought, feeling like such a loser. Of course, one-night stands are no big deal. I don't know why I'm making them into something they're not. Maybe I'd really feel a little better after a night of good sex. The thought sounds a bit funny, so I smile to myself.

I don't talk to myself anymore. I used to do that before, as a kid, but mostly when I needed to boost my own confidence. It was one of those mirror talking kind of things. You speak to yourself in the mirror, pretending it's someone else, but you know it's not. It's not like I'm crazy or anything. At least, I don't think so.

I wonder now what my childhood self would tell my college self. Tsk, tsk, tsk. I think those would be the exact words. With that tone of complete and utter disappointment.

I take another sip, closing my eyes, and feeling the last rays of the dying sun on my face. At least, the weather is nice, and the coffee is delicious. You have to be content with the little things. I used to do that before, but somehow, I feel like I've lost myself. I've lost that inner guide which I always had, and I always trusted. Now, I feel at the mercy of the winds around me and I have no idea where I'm sailing off to.

"This seat taken?"

I suddenly hear a voice. A strangely familiar voice.

When I open my eyes, it's him. Him.

"Twice in several days? What are the odds of that," I tell him, realizing only then that I meant to think it, not say it out loud.

Luckily, he smiles. "Right?" He nods. "What are the odds?"

Without waiting to be told whether the seat is taken, he sits down next to me, lowering his backpack on the ground next to his feet.

I inhale deeply, realizing that it's not his usual cologne. Usual cologne. A little voice reminds me that after all this time, how could I know his usual cologne? He's not the same person I dated. Heck, I'm not the same person he dated. We're two strangers who happened to stumble onto each other on campus. Nothing else.

"I hope you don't need to relieve yourself," I say, trying to break the ice, but the moment I say it out loud, I wish I could take it back. It sounds like I've crossed some invisible line. Maybe it would have been a good joke if we were friends, but we were nothing, just acquaintances.

Then, he smiles, assuring me silently that I'm overthinking things again.

"No, relax," he chuckles. "That... that wasn't my finest moment."

"Not really," I shake my head, unable to smile. "But you had a good excuse. No..." I purposely stop talking, allowing him to continue.

"Free toilets," he finishes my thought, grinning.

He shows me that row of pearly whites I fell for before, but now, everything about him seems more manly, more muscular. I look at him, trying to find out where that guy I dated disappeared off to. He somehow got exchanged for this young man I see before me.

And honestly, I can't say that I don't like what I'm seeing. His arms are bulging from his sleeves, veins etched all along the inside. His fingers are long, and I remember how he used to intertwine them with mine.

I remind myself that it's dangerous to think about the past. Way too dangerous. So, I focus on the present moment.

"What are you doing here?" I ask, knowing that this isn't his usual hangout, otherwise I would have noticed him before.

"I just needed a breather," he says with a sigh, gazing at the setting sun, and the explosion of colors on the horizon.

"From all the girls chasing you about?" Once again, my tongue is faster than my brain. I try to bite my tongue, but it was too late.

He turns to me, a bit surprised to hear me ask that question. "I feel like everyone wants a piece of me," he suddenly says. "And it's tiring me out sometimes. Is that weird?"

I hesitate to answer. But then I figure, he asked for my opinion.

"No," I assure him. "Everyone needs some time to themselves. Whether or not they're the most popular player."

He smiles gratefully. Once again, I remind myself that I don't want to get entangled in what ifs and the memory of what used to be. This is the here and now.

Suddenly, I hear Rachel's voice in my mind, telling me it's OK to have some fun. I look at Callum, and I realize that sleeping with him would be a more comfortable one-night stand, because I've already slept with him before. I know his body, and he knows mine. There would be no unpleasant surprises. We would just... be revisiting old material.

I smile to myself at the comment. He smiles back, and I immediately blush.

"You like to enjoy the sunset on your own?" he asks. I'm wondering if that was his way of asking whether or not I'm seeing someone, but I ignore the question, and instead, offer an answer he wasn't asking for.

"Rachel, my roommate is having someone over," I explain. "I am to stay outside until she calls me telling me the coast is clear."

He frowns, looking worried. "You'll stay out all night?"

"Of course not," I shake my head. "I'll just finish this," I show him my coffee, "then, I'll head to the library. It's open all night. Besides, I'm hoping she won't take all night."

"Does she usually take all night?" he asks, and instantly, I flare up.

"Well, you could go there and see for yourself," I tell him, sounding a little more upset than I wished I was.

"No, that's not what I meant," he smiles, waving his hands defensively at the level of his chest. "I'm asking because I honestly don't feel OK leaving you alone, knowing you can't go home."

"I'll be fine," I assure him. "This coffee should keep me up for hours and I'll just do some reading at the library. There's no safer place on campus than a library."

OK, at this point I'm talking nonsense, but I feel all tongue tied around him, remembering why it was I fell in love with him in the first place.

"No," he shakes his head at me, "I still don't feel OK."

"You don't have to feel OK," I remind him. "I'm not your responsibility."

Pride takes over, and I want to tell him a few other things, which have rested deeply in my soul, things I thought were buried and forgotten, but I see now they aren't. It's a strange feeling, having a war rage on inside of you, when you have no idea what to do with yourself. So, you try to follow your gut. It should know what to do... hopefully.

"I know," he says, and I feel like that's not what I wanted him to say.

But I also don't know what I wanted him to say.

Ugh, this is so confusing. I wish we never stumbled onto each other. Maybe that would have been the best.

"Listen," he starts, scratching the back of his neck. "I know this might sound weird, but... would you like to come to my place instead of the library while you wait for your roommate to call you?"

He catches me completely off guard with that suggestion. My pride roars violently inside of me, urging me to stand up, slap him for assuming I'd do any such thing and just walk away.

But I do no such thing. I can't. I don't want to.

The thing is, I want to go with him. I want to have one night of passion with him. I want to prove Rachel wrong, that sex itself won't help me much. It may help her, but I need more than just sex. So, maybe this might prove my point. And I might have some fun in the meantime. As for the consequences of this thoughtless endeavor... well, I'll cross that bridge when I get to it.

I lift my eyebrow at him, pondering. Actually, I've already made up my mind, but I don't want him to know this.

"Do you have any books?" I ask. I'm guessing no. What jock has books?

"No," he shakes his head, and I feel a pang of disappointment. I somehow remember he had a few books in his room before. Or maybe I'm mistaken. "But I have a Kindle. You can see what books I have downloaded, or you can download any you like and read them while you wait."

I smile at his suggestion. Maybe that's not such a bad idea.

Maybe Rachel is right. Maybe I need to unwind a little, let go of my inhibitions and just allow myself to have some fun. I know Callum. I know his touch, his kisses. It will be like going back to some old forgotten place where you used to vacation a long time ago. And this will be another little vacation. Just that. Nothing more.

I can do this. I just have to close my heart and remind myself that this changes nothing. He is still the asshole who dumped me for football. But that doesn't mean I can't have some fun with this asshole. And then go about my merry way.

I almost chuckle to myself. This doesn't sound like me at all. It sounds like Rachel. Maybe she's been rubbing off on me. That wouldn't be such a bad thing at all.

"OK," I finally say, downing my coffee, then throwing the paper cup in the trash. "Lead the way."

Chapter Six

Callum

I don't know why, but I'm nervous. Elsie hasn't been in my apartment before. While we were dating, I was housed in one of the worst dorm rooms in the whole campus, and she said nothing when she came there for the first time. All she did was look at me.

This time, however, she's not looking at me. She's curious about the place, as she enters the living room and stands right in the middle of the room.

"It's nice," she says a little impassively. I can't tell if she's saying it just to be polite or not.

She walks around the room, looking at the art on the wall.

"I never figured you for the artsy type," she smiles, turning around to face me.

"I'm not," I shrug. "I didn't decorate the place. I just get to live in it while I'm... the star quarterback, I guess."

She looks at me but says nothing. When I say those words, it feels like I'm mocking something. Her? Our relationship? I don't know but saying it out loud doesn't really feel good.

"You want something to drink?" I ask her. "I have beer, wine, some Coke."

"Coke is fine," she tells me.

I nod, disappearing in the kitchen. I wonder if inviting her back to my place was a smart idea. I don't want her to think that I'm trying to take advantage of the situation. Because I'm not. At least, I don't think so.

I'm overthinking things, and that's not good. So, I just grab the Coke, and bring it to her.

"Thanks," she smiles as she accepts it.

We both sit on the sofa, and I feel the tension around us is too thick, I could cut it with a knife.

"You want me to get you the Kindle?" I offer.

"Not yet," she says, surprising me. "Why don't you play us some music?"

She flicks the can open and takes a sip, not taking her eyes off me. I grab the remote for the TV and play us some slower hip-hop.

I feel like there are so many questions I want to ask her, to see how she's been doing all this time, but there's that barrier I can't get past. I know what I need to say. I have to apologize, I have to take responsibility for the fucked-up way we broke up, and only then can I–

But before my mind can even start processing what's happened, I feel her lips on mine. Her eyes are closed. She always kissed with closed eyes. But I loved to watch her.

I don't know where all this came from, but I'm not questioning it. Her lips awakened long forgotten desires, and my stomach explodes, heat traveling down all the way to my cock and the bundle of nerves there.

She opens her mouth for me more, sucking my tongue. I groan with pleasure.

I know I should go slow, but I can't control myself. It's like there's been a dam somewhere inside of me, and now, all the water is flooding out.

I pull her t-shirt over her head. Her bra is peach colored, lacy, transparent. I can see her erect nipples through it. I go over the thin fabric with the tips of my fingers and she moans in reply.

Memories wash over me, instantly, electrifying me. The moment I touch the heat of her skin, it's as if no time has passed since the last time we slept together. I am stunned by this. I just go with the flow, as our bodies find each other again. I have no idea how this is happening at all, but I'm not questioning anything.

I can feel the heat emanating from her body, intense, completely taking me over. Within seconds, we are both naked, our clothes flying about the room, ending on the floor.

I drop down to my knees, spreading her legs. She writhes underneath my touch, trembling. I know I shouldn't feel proud that I still have that effect on her, but I do. She closes her eyes. I get closer to her, licking her slit, parting her folds slowly, tantalizingly. Her fingers find my hair, digging into it, clutching at it. I slide my tongue into her, thrusting in and out slowly at first, picking up the rhythm.

She bucks against my mouth, losing control the faster I go. I add my thumb, pressing at her swollen clit, as my tongue keeps sliding into her faster and faster, with steady pressure.

Her entire body is convulsing, trembling. Her fingers are digging harder into my hair. She's pulling me closer to her, as if she's afraid I might pull away. But I have no such intention. Her hips move upward. She's holding me exactly where she wants me. I can feel her desire in the way she clenches at me, in the way she's breathing, moaning my name. The sight of her is so good, I feel my dick beading up cum, and she hasn't even touched me. I can't remember the last time I was so hot for a girl, so eager to be inside of her. But I don't want to rush it. I want to pleasure her first.

I keep burying my tongue inside of her deep, lapping up the wetness that oozed out of her, as our juices mix. I murmur against her pussy lips, swollen and tender. She moans loudly, a guttural sound. I don't remember her ever making that sound before.

"Don't stop..." she begs me, and her words make me even hotter for her.

I grab her hips and pull them closer to me. She trembles as I move away, gasping, but I don't allow her even a moment of rest. I sink a finger inside of her slowly, enjoying how wet and ready she is for me. I work it in and out of her. How it glides... The wet sounds echo all around us, and I know she's coming undone. It's only a matter of time before she explodes. But I want her even more turned on. I want her to never forget this night.

I add a second finger, and she tenses up a bit. I slow down the rhythm.

"Don't stop..." she repeats, as her body relaxes again.

I curl my fingers inside of her, hitting the exact right spot, then I flick my tongue over her clit again. I suck at it, moving my fingers in and out of her, giving her exactly what she wants, deeper and deeper, filling her up. I enhance the rhythm, and that is more than she can take. She is thrusting against me, begging me to keep going, and I comply.

Suddenly, her entire body stiffens, and I can feel the palpitations deep inside of her. I keep sucking at her clit, until finally the grip she has on my hair is released. I give her a few moments to regain her senses, planting soft kisses on the inside of her thigh. Then, I pull away and she opens her eyes.

She is following me with her eyes as I disappear in the bedroom and come back with a condom wrapper. I tear it open and roll the condom onto my cock, which is already throbbing with need. She stays in that spread-legged position, and I just want to drop down on my knees before her again.

But instead, I settle between her legs, grabbing my cock at the base, and adjusting it right in front of her pussy, which is glistening with her juices. I slide inside effortlessly, that lingering desire exploding all around me. I sigh once I am fully inside of her.

Our eyes lock. She doesn't have them closed now. She is smiling. I smile back, lowering my lips to hers. She wraps her legs around me, locking us together, pulling me closer to her, showing me she wants me even deeper.

"You feel so good," I murmur against her lips.

I can't keep still any longer. I start to move, thrusting in and out of her. My movements are steady and measured at first. I can still control myself... up to a certain point. Her fingers rake against my back, and it makes me go wild, making my strokes faster, more needy, more desperate for her. I'm losing control at this point, just giving in to what she wanted, what she started.

Our breaths are filling the room. The heat is unbearable. We're both so close. I want her to come again, and again, but I can't hold on any longer. I implode instantly, as a wave of unbearable pleasure washes over me. I pump my cock several times more, as she clings to me, digging her fingers into my back, and a moment later, her body mirrors my motions, trembling underneath me.

Her insides are palpitating, as we're both mindless after our orgasm, lying almost boneless against each other. I pull out from her, going to the bathroom, to wash up. By the time I'm back, she's already dressed, looking at her phone. She lifts her gaze to meet mine. I expect her to say something, although I'm not sure what. This was so unexpected. It completely took me off guard. But I'm not the one to complain.

"Do you maybe wanna order dinner or something?" I offer, feeling ridiculous for the first time ever after sex. Not because anything was wrong, because it wasn't, but simply because I have no idea how I got where I am now.

"No, thanks," she says, sounding perfectly fine. Well, at least that. She puts her phone in her bag, then continues. "Rachel sent me a message. I can go back." She slips her bag onto her shoulder and heads over to me. She kisses me on the cheek, and I still don't get anything.

"Don't take this the wrong way," she tells me. "It was just... for fun. Don't worry, I won't bug you or anything."

With those words she heads to the door, and I rush after her.

"Wait," I tell her. "I can drive you back."

"No," she tells me, already unlocking the door and pressing the doorknob. "I'll call a cab. See ya."

And just like that, she closes the door, leaving me alone, completely happy and completely fucked up at the same time. I'm just wondering which one of those two emotions to focus on right now.

Chapter Seven

Elsie

I didn't tell Rachel where I was. For some reason, the words just didn't come, although I felt a few times as if they were on the tip of my tongue. Yet, I didn't mention anything. She thought I just spent that time at the library, as I'm doing now. Only now, she doesn't have anyone back in our dorm room. I'm just in need of some solitary time.

I have barely glanced at the book in front of me for the past half an hour. If anyone was watching, they'd think I was a horrible reader, not finishing a single page in thirty minutes. But it feels nice to just be alone with my thoughts, which are all a jumbled mess right now.

It was just a one-off thing. I keep reminding myself of this. And the more times I repeat this, the more I'm starting to believe it. Of course, it felt good, because I did it with someone I know in that way, someone who already knows my body as well. I'm guessing if I did it with someone I don't know or some acquaintance, there was a fifty-fifty chance of it being a hit or miss. This time, I assumed I'd get good sex, and I did. Now, I can tell Rachel that I did. I got laid. She can get off my back, we can go back to me hating being here and figuring out what it is exactly I want to do with myself and my life, because I have no freakin' idea.

I sigh at the book, which is not beckoning me to keep reading it at all. In fact, I'd rather just put it back and find something else, anything else, to occupy myself. Suddenly, I think of my parents. I know how disappointed they would be to hear that I'm regretting most of the choices I've made up to this point. When they were both my age, they knew exactly what they wanted to do with their lives. Me? I feel like I know less than when I started out on this journey.

I sigh heavily to myself, burying my face into my hands. They're coming over to see me soon, and that thought both excites me, and terrifies me. I'll be happy to see them, as always. But at the same time, they'll ask me how my studies are going, and I'll have to lie to them. I've never lied to my parents. Not once. I felt like we always had a good connection, and I could come to them with anything that was bothering me. This time, however, I feel like they might not understand. They might be disappointed with me, and I'm not sure I'd be able to handle that.

When I finally remove my hands from my face, I realize someone is sitting opposite me at the table. The big green lamp to my right is keeping most of his face in the shadows, but I can see enough of him to recognize him instantly.

"What are you doing here?" I whisper, leaning closer to him.

He does the same. "Rachel told me you're here."

"So?" I frown, wondering what he wants. I told him last night that I don't want anything from him.

Maybe an apology for the way he dumped me, but I like to think that I'm over that.

Or not. I can't really know. This is a difficult time for me, and all I wanted was to have some fun, but now he's here, wanting God knows what.

"I told you that I don't expect anything from you," I repeat under my breath.

"I also don't want anything from you," he replies.

"Why are you here then?" I ask, raising my eyebrow at him.

"I don't know."

His response is so sudden, so genuine, and something tells me he's not lying. He's not trying to impress me. He's here because... he doesn't even know why he's here. I can totally relate to that.

"Come on," I get up, closing my book and putting it back into my backpack.

"Where?" he asks.

"Shhh," I press my finger to my lips. "Didn't you know this is a library?"

In half an hour, we reach a nearby lookout point. I don't know why I told him to drive here. Maybe because the lights that are overlooking the city below us feel somehow soothing. They're so little, but their light is so strong. I want to believe that I might be like that as well. Little, but strong.

We stay in the car, a bit further away from another car, which already has steamed up windows. I noticed as we passed them by. But of course, you give others some privacy in places such as this one, and you expect the same.

"Are you sure this is where you want to be right now?" he asks, sounding a bit incredulous.

"I know, weird, right?" I nod, looking ahead at the lights flickering. "I like this spot." Then, I realize he might think I like it because I come here often to fuck someone, and that's the last thing that's on my mind right now. I just want... the lights to soothe me. "It's not what you think," I add quickly. "I like the lights."

"The lights?" he repeats, gazing at them as well.

"Yeah, I mean, just look at them," I shrug. "They keep flickering, little and so bright. Don't mind me, I'm being ridiculous."

"It's OK," he says softly, not taking his eyes off the lights. "We can just stay here a while. Whatever you want."

For some reason, I expect him to give me that apology that I've been due, but he doesn't. He just stops talking. And I keep fighting myself on this. I keep reminding myself that I am not determined by any stupid apology that some insignificant guy can give me. But then again, I feel like I deserve closure. Everyone does.

I sigh, but there is little relief. Still, I feel less burdened than back at the library. I'm not expecting anything. I don't want anything. But I guess I should want things. Everyone wants things, right? Well, I don't know what I want or why I'm here, with him of all people.

"I had fun," he tells me suddenly. "Last night."

Sure? I don't really know what to say to that. So, I say nothing.

I notice that he's not looking at the lights anymore. He's looking at me. He's burning a hole right in my cheek. Then, I also remember last night. I remember how I kissed him first, breathlessly, without thinking. It was not me who did it. It was some other Elsie, the Elsie who is always kept under lock and key, because she is dangerous. She does what she wants, without even considering the consequences. That Elsie was exactly the one who told him to drive here.

And suddenly, she takes the reigns again. I allow her.

Coming undone in someone's arms is how I can forget all about my problems. Callum is here. He wants this as much as I do. One more time couldn't hurt... could it?

Before I can consider it any longer, he kisses me first this time. I reciprocate in the same way as he did last night. My arms fly to him, as I cup his cheeks with the palms of my hands, bringing him closer to me. His kisses are ravenous, as if he wants to eat me up alive. I know that feeling. I am equally starved for someone's attention.

He quickly unbuttons my jeans and slides his hand inside my panties. I hiss against his lips loudly, but he suppresses my moan with his tongue, licking me, biting me, sucking me, bringing me to that same incredible sensation from before. His fingers slide inside of me quickly, in one go.

"You are so wet, Elsie..." he tells me, and the sound of my name on his lips drives me crazy.

I bring myself closer to him. I could come just from his fingers inside of me and his voice whispering in my ear, but I want more, and I don't want to wait.

"I want you inside me, now," I tell him.

In response, he sinks his finger deeper inside of me, and I groan in heat. He curls his fingers, and the angle is absolutely bliss. Every part of my body is reacting to him in a way I never even thought it could react to anybody. I bite my lip, thinking how glorious it will be when he slides inside of me.

Then, he pulls out his finger, and reaches into his pocket. I take off only one of my trouser legs and slide my panties down the same way. When he looks at me again, he chuckles, and I chuckle back. I have no idea why we're laughing, but it feels so liberating, so unburdening.

He adjusts himself over me, lowering the seat behind me into a reclining position. The seat bumps down, and he falls right on top of me.

"Sorry," he says, again chuckling, his voice so endearing.

"It's OK," I assure him, smiling.

Our eyes lock again, like the previous night, and I feel a pang of something I can't explain. Maybe it's best not to think about it too much. I'll be overthinking again. I don't want that. Especially not now. There is only one thing I want now, only one thing I need.

He takes himself in his hand and finds my entrance easily. He makes this cute, stupid face, as he plunges into me, and pleasure washes over me. I close my eyes, completely surrendering to the moment. I hear his ragged breathing right by my ear, as he keeps sliding in and out of me. He doesn't start off slowly. We're both out of control, and we can't take it slowly. Not now.

I feel my entire body tightening around him, drawing him inside deeper and faster, needing more and more with each thrust. I feel like the whole world has disappeared around us, and we're the only two people left as we fill our car with hot air and moaning breaths. Nothing else exists but this moment and the two of us.

He slams into me forcefully, deeply. The angle is perfect and he's hitting just the right spot.

"I'm cumming," he tells me against my ear, and his admission quickens my own desperate need to cum.

My inner muscles all clamp, spasming around him. He pumps a few more times, sliding into me hard. I feel his cock palpitating in me, and at that very moment, I close my eyes under the onslaught of my own orgasm. It ripples through me like a thunderstorm, when his head slumps down onto my neck, and we both find it difficult to regain our breaths.

A few moments later, he pulls out and I get dressed, wiggling back into my panties and jeans. Strangely, the silence doesn't feel awkward. In fact, I welcome it. It allows me to relax, for my body to regain its senses and come back to reality.

We're both gazing at the lights, which I still can't seem to find inside of me, but rather outside. For the time being, that's enough.

I listen to the sound of his breathing, as I keep reminding myself that this will be the last time. No more. Because I'm not sure where we might go from there.

From here, I can still see a path and that path is away from him. I can still keep myself under control, my own emotions which are a mess, but I can handle them. But I know I can't cross the line a third time with him. It might be too much. Heck, this might be too much, but all I need is a talk with Rachel. She'll set me straight, as she always does.

As for now, I'll enjoy the silence and the lights.

Chapter Eight

Callum

I always hated hospitals. Ever since my grandad ended up in one, and despite what everyone was telling me, I had a feeling that he would not leave the hospital alive. Even as a seven-year-old, I could understand that just from the way all those wires and tubes were poking out of him, and that constant pinging noise from the machines in his room. He stayed positive until the last moment when he lost his battle to lung cancer. Even while coughing, and barely able to breathe, he still had enough strength to smile and hold me by the hand, his eyes telling me not to worry. And the seven-year-old me worried until the very last moment.

Now, that is what hospitals remind me of. For some people, hospitals are a place of hope. This is what we tell kids. When someone needs to go to the hospital, they go there because hospitals are places where they cure people. They never tell you that sometimes, hospitals are also places where people go to die, and all hospitals can do is just ease the suffering.

I'm seated in the waiting room, trying not to make any eye contact. Although it's hard to just keep to yourself and stare at your own sneakers.

I rub my elbow instinctively, blaming my injury from a month ago for this unpleasant visit. I kept telling my coach that my arm feels OK, but he still sent me for a checkup.

I look around against all better judgment. There is a young mother with a kid sitting a little to my right. The kid has his head in her lap, and she is caressing his hair. His cheeks are blazing red. Maybe he's got a fever. Every once in a while, she would lower her head to his, giving him a soft kiss on the cheek.

There is an elderly couple next to them. The man is holding the woman's hand in his own. She seems more worried than he is, while he smiles benevolently at her.

There is a multitude of different people here, different ages, all here because they have to be, not because they want to be. I'm just hoping that I won't have to wait too long. I look at the other end of the waiting room, and for a moment I think I recognize a man there.

I squint, as if that might sharpen my vision, and it does. The man doesn't look at me, and I see only the profile of his face. He is bending forward, his elbows resting on his knees. I notice that there is a small folder on a seat next to him.

I try to figure out why he looks so familiar. Usually, I would just look away, but right now, there is nothing else to do and I want to take my mind off the unpleasant fact that I'm at a hospital.

So, I discreetly stare at the man, trying to remember where I could have seen him. He's not one of my professors. I would have recognized him already. It doesn't seem like it's anyone I'd know off campus. Maybe a scout? I try to rewind all the scout faces I've seen and met in the last two years, but this man doesn't fit anywhere in there either.

The more time passes, the more intrigued I am. He finally pulls himself backward, leaning against his chair. He is still with half of his face away from me.

I shake my head, trying to shift my focus. I don't want anyone to notice me staring at a stranger in the waiting room of the hospital. So, I get up and walk to the bathroom. I take a quick leak, wash my hands, and splash some cold water on my face, too. I stare at myself in the mirror, looking a bit paler than usual. I quickly pat myself dry, then head outside.

Just as I push the door open towards the outside, I feel that it slams against a hard surface, and a bunch of papers scatter all about. I close the door, only then realizing that I slammed the door against someone, and that someone was exactly the man I had been staring down for the last fifteen minutes or so.

He's bent over his documents, picking them all up.

"Oh, I'm so sorry, man," I tell him, proceeding to do the same.

I start gathering all the papers, trying not to look at what it says, but the mind is a treacherous thing. Even if you don't want to read what it says, because you know it's private and not for your eyes, your brain goes ahead and does it, nonetheless. I immediately recognize the blood tests used to look for small pieces of cancer cells' genetic material. I had no idea I even knew what any of these tests were, but again... a mind is a treacherous thing. It remembers best the things you want to forget, just like my own grandfather's tests and blood work results. I remember my mom leaving them on a desk one time, and the curious bugger that I was, I read it. I've been able to read since I was five, although I never felt it brought me much benefit. Especially in cases such as this one.

Both me and the guy get up at the same time, our eyes clashing against each other. Suddenly, it hits me. I recognize him instantly.

"Mr. Medina," I address Elsie's father.

He looks at me as if he doesn't recognize me.

"I'm Callum, Callum Holland," I explain, scratching the back of my neck. "We met once or twice, while I was dating your daughter, Elsie."

It takes him a few moments longer before his eyes glow up in recognition. Or he's just being nice and pretends to recognize me. In either case, I appreciate not being left to just hang.

"Of course, Callum," he nods, smiling, offering me his hand. "Sorry I didn't recognize you immediately. It's been a while."

"Yeah, it has," I nod, shaking his hand cordially. I offer him the documents I picked up for him, and I can see the embarrassment in his eyes.

"Thank you," he tells me. He stares at the papers, not even trying to hide them. I wonder if he knows I glanced at them. Probably. Otherwise, this moment wouldn't be so awkward.

Now I'm sure I should have just sat in my place, waiting to be called out.

"So, uhm, Callum, how's school?" he asks, and I know he's doing it just to be polite. He wants this conversation to end just as much as I do, but it'd be rude to just go our separate ways, now that we sort of found each other again.

Meeting Elsie's parents was never something I planned on doing, and I don't think she planned it either. I remember us being on a date, and her parents ended up surprising her with an early visit, and her roommate told them where we were having dinner. One thing led to another, and it became a family dinner of sorts. I can't say I didn't enjoy it.

The John Medina I met was cracking jokes the entire evening, leading the conversation, but not in an annoying way. His wife would constantly put her hand on his, trying to get him to stop embarrassing Elsie with stories from her childhood, but in reality, she enjoyed them as much as we all did. Only Elsie pouted a little, especially when he told the story how she taught their cat to use the litter box, by pooping in the box herself when she was only seven. I guess everyone does something monumental when they're seven.

The John Medina I see now before me looks like a washed-out version of that man. An unhealthy version.

"School's fine," I say.

"You play some sports, don't you?" he asks.

"Yeah, football," I nod, smiling.

"How's that workin' out for ya?" he continues good-naturedly.

"Great," I nod. "I might be getting a shot to play in the big league soon."

"I'm glad to hear that," he tells me.

This is where the conversation dies out, because we don't really want to talk. If we had stumbled onto each other anywhere else in the whole world, the conversation could have flowed in a whole different direction.

"Listen," he says, sounding a little apprehensive, his voice down to almost a whisper as we're a bit away from the waiting room, but there are still people passing us by. "I don't know if you're still in touch with Elsie or not..."

"Here and there," I say, shrugging.

"Yeah, well..." he pauses, as if searching for the right words. Then, he finally finds them. "I would appreciate it if you didn't mention that we met here."

There it is. The situation must be even worse than I assumed, if he's asking me this. But of course, I can only comply.

"Your secret is safe with me, Mr. Medina," I say, then frown, realizing that's probably the worst thing I could have said under the circumstances. I look at him apologetically. "Sorry, I didn't mean anything by it. I just thought– "

"It's OK," he smiles, patting me on the shoulder. "And I'm fine. This is just... the doctors just want to double check, nothing else. But I don't want to worry her. Elsie's got enough on her plate, as I'm sure you do, too. The last thing she needs is to worry over nothing."

"Of course, Mr. Medina," I nod.

"I really appreciate that, Callum," he adds offering me his hand once again. I shake it firmly, feeling his clammy palm against mine. "Well, I'd better go back and wait to be called."

"Yeah, same," I reply, allowing him to retreat first, back to his place.

I wait a few moments, opting instead to go down the hallway in the opposite direction and grab a coffee from the machine. I'm not in any particular mood for a drink, but I don't think I can face that man immediately at the waiting room.

As I'm waiting for my coffee to stop being poured into a plastic cup, I can't help but think that I somehow imposed on this man's most private moment here. I slammed the door against him, making him drop his file, and I saw his blood work results, which he would not have shown me under any other circumstances. Everything about this is wrong. And yet, all I can think about is Elsie.

I doubt her dad would ask me to keep this a secret if it was merely just a routine checkup. Once again, I have become a part of her family, at least for a little while, without the slightest intention of imposing upon any of them.

When my coffee is finally done, I inhale deeply, then head back to the waiting room. I exhale with relief upon seeing that her father isn't there. I sit back down. The kid next to me is up now and is looking much better. His mother is smiling, telling him something which is making him smile in return.

I feel hopeful seeing them like that, but the truth is still there, lurking behind me, with its cold talons. Hospitals are a place for the ill, but not everyone can get better, and there is nothing you can do about that.

Chapter Nine

Elsie

I glance at my watch, hoping that I'm not late. I still have five minutes to spare, but I still hasten my step, as I turn around the corner. I can already see the restaurant in the distance, with its green, shaded garden. This is where we arranged to meet, and honestly, I don't remember the last time I felt this excited.

I look at myself in the shop window as I'm passing by, adjusting my ponytail a little, then continuing on my way. Before I even reach the restaurant, I see my mom waving at me. She noticed me before I noticed them, not that this surprises me much.

"Elsie!" she shouts, and a few people look at her weirdly, but she doesn't care at all. She keeps waving at me, although I see her plain as daylight.

I start chuckling as I wave back. Dad is sitting next to her, smiling as well. I reach them quickly, and immediately fall into the endlessly loving embrace of my mother. I inhale deeply, my mind immediately overtaken by scents that evoke childhood memories of pure joy. I close my eyes, relishing the moment. It feels like neither of us wants to let go of the other, as we stand there hugging.

"Alright, alright," dad interrupts our tender moment, and mom reluctantly lets go of me, only for me to be enshrouded into another pair of strong, muscular arms.

I hug my dad back, feeling less of him. He kisses both my cheeks, also eventually releasing me reluctantly.

"You lost weight?" I ask, wondering why I felt less of him somehow while we hugged. Usually, he had much more to work with around his back and belly.

"I don't know," he shrugs. "Ask your mom."

"Me?" Mom's eyes widen in surprise, her clear blue eyes in which I saw my own reflection so many times.

"Haven't you been cooking some healthy food lately?" he teases.

"Oh, yeah," she chuckles. "Guilty as charged."

We all chuckle, and I find my seat between the two of them. I can't seem to take my eyes off them. I saw them last a couple of months ago, but for some reason, it feels like ages. I don't know whether it's because of everything that's happened, but it feels good to be around people who love you unconditionally.

"How was your trip?" I ask, as dad puts a menu in front of me, but I don't open it yet. I want to savor this moment for as long as I can.

"Oh, fine," dad shrugs. "The usual."

"We started early yesterday," mom explains.

"Yesterday?" I repeat. "I thought you were coming today."

Mom and dad lock gazes for a moment, then dad explains. "Well, you know how much your mom loves shopping, so I thought I'd surprise her with a day of visiting her favorite shops in town."

"Why didn't you tell me you were here?" I wonder. "I could have joined you."

"Oh, no, sweetheart," mom waves her hand at me. "We know how busy you are with your studies and everything. We didn't want to take up too much of your time. We're just happy you could have lunch with us today."

"Are you returning today?" I ask.

"Yes," she nods. "That was the plan. You know we don't like to be away from our home for too long."

"I know," I smile, feeling a sense of homesickness overwhelm me.

At that moment, the waiter comes, and my dad glances at us. "I think we're ready to order."

I skim through the menu as my parents make their order, and once we're done, the waiter retires.

"How are things back home?" I ask, realizing that I'm desperate to hear whatever they have to tell me.

I remember hating small town life as a teenager. I couldn't wait to get the heck out of there and start my new life in the big city. When that finally happened, I felt like I was in some crazy dream, and I might wake up any moment. But that didn't happen. Every morning, I kept waking up and I was still there, still living my dream. Only then, my dream started to change, and little by little, it wasn't my dream anymore. It was someone else's.

Now, looking at my parents and listening to them talk about the simple life, and how they know everyone in town where they grew up, how they can always tell old John at the grocery store that they'll pay tomorrow if they didn't have enough cash on them, I feel like maybe this was all a big mistake, me coming here.

But I can't tell them that. I can't tell the most important people in my life that I'm afraid I made a horrible mistake, and I don't know how to fix it. Not from where I'm standing.

So, I keep listening to my mother's voice, and the sound of my father's laughter, as they tell me about our dogs, and cat which had a litter of eight kittens, and our chickens and ducks, and the fact that our cat is too focused on something else now, so they have mice again.

"I don't hate mice," my mom says. "They're kinda cute, if you think about it. But rats..." She shivers at the very mention of rats. "I hate rats."

"I think we might have rats as well," dad adds gravely, reaching for his fizzy water and taking a sip, his eyes focused on mom.

Her eyes are as wide as bicycle wheels. "What?" she gasps. "You're joking. Please tell me you're joking."

"No," he shakes his head. "I saw some droppings in the barn. To tell ya honestly, I think it's rats' dropping."

Mom is taking him completely seriously, but I can see that small twitch in the corner of his mouth. He's about to burst out into laughter, telling her it's all a joke. But he wants to keep it going for as long as he can, because mom has always been gullible.

"John," mom says his name as seriously as she can, giving him the evil eye, when he finally can't resist any longer and starts chuckling. She immediately realizes that he's been pulling her leg all along. "Oh, you are just the worst person ever!"

He's still laughing, as he reaches for her hand, and leans closer to her to kiss her. "But you love me, nonetheless. Admit it."

She pretends to sigh heavily, shaking her head at him. "You're lucky I love you, because who else would love you?"

"No one," he confirms. "The only people I want to love me are right here, at this table."

I almost cry at those words, and I have no idea why. Maybe it's stupid PMS hitting ahead of time, making me overly emotional, and I blink heavily, trying to keep tears at bay. I finally manage to do it, and the food arrives at that very moment.

"That looks delicious," he comments on my spaghetti carbonara.

"You want to try it?" I offer.

"No, I'm a man of simple tastes," he says, gesturing at his hamburger and fries.

"You could eat healthier, you know," mom frowns, then grabs her fork and pokes her Caesar salad with it.

The rest of our lunch passes by quickly. Too quickly. When I glance at my watch, I realize that I promised Rachel I would meet her for a study session, as we're getting ready for an exam next week.

"Do you have to go, darling?" mom asks.

"I really don't want to go," I say, a little saddened that the time with them just flew by. It felt like just a blink, and now I already have to leave them.

"It's OK, darling," mom says. "We understand you've got obligations. And we're happy that you do. You have no idea how proud we are every time one of our neighbors asks us about you, and we always say where you are and what you're studying."

I can see the glimmer of pride in her motherly eyes, and I know I can't tell them any of my fears or concerns. Hearing that would devastate them. I would disappoint them. I would take away that feeling of pride from them. And I fear nothing would ever be the same between us. I can't possibly risk that.

"Yes," I nod, not really sure what else to say.

"Your studies are going well, I hope?" Dad interferes into the conversation.

"Oh yeah," I nod again. "Perfect. Couldn't be better," I grin, making sure not to overdo it. I just can't go into much detail. Just keep it simple. A simple lie is easily controlled. A more complicated one, where you offer too many details, make you get entangled in your own words and you end up completely lost.

"We're so glad to hear that," mom gushes, reaching for my hand.

Her touch is warm and loving, and a part of me just wants to fall into her arms and admit everything, hoping for the best. But I know what they sacrificed to get me where I am, and I can't fail them.

"Do you need us to drive you back to campus?" dad offers, as he lifts his hand in the air to call the waiter for the bill.

"No, I'm fine," I smile. "It's just a ten-minute walk. And the weather is so nice."

"It really is," mom agrees. "Maybe next time, we could all go somewhere together, for the weekend. If you have time, of course."

I feel a hand clenching at my heart and seizing it tightly every time mom says something so endearing and loving. Almost as if I don't deserve those words from her.

"I think that's a great idea, mom," I smile, my lip trembling.

"Lovely," she claps her hands together in joy. "We'll arrange it for next time."

Dad pays the bill, and together we walk out of the restaurant, stopping at a nearby traffic lights, where we are to go our own separate ways.

"We're parked over there," dad points in the opposite direction from the one I'm going to. "You sure you don't want us to drop you off?"

"I'm good, dad, really," I assure him.

"Well, alright then," he says, wrapping his arms around me. I inhale deeply, burying my nose into the collar of his shirt. Then, it's mom's turn to hug me, and I grip at her, like a dying man grips at a life preserver belt.

"Is everything OK, darling?" mom asks.

It's amazing how moms always know that something is wrong, especially when you're doing your best to hide it from them.

"Yeah, mom," I assure her, smiling as widely as I can without making it look fake. "I'm just so happy I saw you guys and I wish we could spend more time together."

"Oh, darling," she caresses my face with the palm of her hand. "You'll come visit soon, won't you?"

"Of course," I nod.

"And we'll also find an excuse to take a short trip to the city again," dad winks at me. "OK, champ. Be good and call us, OK?"

"Of course," I repeat.

Mom hugs me quickly again, and I watch as they walk back to their car. Mom turns around one more time, and that is when I turn around and head in the opposite direction. I feel tears welling in my eyes, and two big ones roll down my cheeks. I allow them.

Maybe I'll manage to get this feeling out of my system before I see Rachel, so I don't have to explain it to her. Although, she's like my mom. She knows when something is wrong. She can sense it, that stupid gut feeling of hers. I wish I had one of those, too. Maybe I wouldn't be in this situation where I am now, if I had it.

Chapter Ten

Callum

My afternoon practice is done, and although I still need to attend one more in the evening, I decide to go home for a quick bite to eat and to pick up a few things, then head out later again.

I'm walking through campus grounds, waving to a few familiar faces, when suddenly I wonder what Elsie is doing. Maybe I could hit her up for a coffee or something.

At this point, I'm not sure what exactly I'm doing, or even why I'm doing it. This secret I found out feels really difficult to carry, but I promised I wouldn't tell her anything. Talk about being in the wrong place at the wrong time. I can't even imagine how the man must be feeling.

But I know he can't have it easy. I didn't see the result properly, but I did recognize a few numbers, and they didn't look good. It's one of those things your mind remembers even when you want to forget. I don't remember exactly how bad they were, but I know it's not good.

I remember his words, urging me not to tell Elsie. But that is the biggest mistake he can make, not have his family around him in this difficult moment. And knowing Elsie, she will be devastated. I know this is my chance to prove to her that she can rely on me, if not as a partner, then at least as a friend. I'll accept that for the time being and prove to her that I'm not the man... no, I'm not the boy who dumped her before.

I keep walking, looking around, realizing that I've spent all this time focusing on the wrong things in life. Ambition is a good thing, I've been told. But it's not good if it comes at the expense of those who truly care about you. And in this short time, I've been popular on campus, but I can't say I've felt that true, deep love. Everything about this world is superficial. One fad substitutes another as quickly as the snap of your fingers.

I still want the things I wanted. I still want to make it and play pro ball, but I feel like I somehow got stuck in this world, while I could have achieved the same thing, only with Elsie by my side. Actually, I might even have achieved more, because now I realize that she would never have held me back. It's not who she is. She would do anything in her power to push me forward. And I was the idiot who couldn't see that. I was the idiot who believed that having a girlfriend, some other priority apart from football would be detrimental to achieving my goal.

At that moment, I see someone walk up to me, straight in the line I'm walking, without the slightest intention of changing her trajectory. When I lift my gaze, I realize it's Maddie. She's already got that wide grin, happy to see me. Only I'm not as happy to see her.

She stops right in front of me, making it impossible for me to pass.

"We gotta stop meeting like this," she purrs. "Someone might think you're stalking me."

I smile, but it's a weak effort. "I'm just walking to my car."

"Heading somewhere?" she asks.

"Yeah, home," I nod.

"Want some company?" She leans closer, and once again, her perfume overpowers me, like someone stuck two fingers up my nostrils and pushed even deeper.

"It's been a long day," I say, trying to be nice. "I just finished practice, and– "

"Then you must be very dirty," she interrupts me. "How about you take me home, and I help you wash yourself off?"

I know any guy would consider himself lucky to get such an invitation. But there is absolutely no reaction from me, in any department, either up or down. It's like I've grown immune to her charms, of which there are many. But she just doesn't do it for me.

"I appreciate the offer," I say, still keeping it nice and polite. "But I already told you how I feel about this."

"That's because you're not giving it a chance," she urges. "I'm sure I could make you change your mind and feel something else."

While I'm sure this might be possibly, I'm still not liking it. There are only two options for me at the moment. I want to either go home alone or spend the rest of the afternoon with Elsie, which I doubt would happen, because I've sent her two messages already, which she ignored. I considered calling, but I don't want to be that guy.

I have no idea if there is even an option of making it with Elsie. I'd like to think there is, but she can be as stubborn as a mule sometimes. And if she's told me she isn't expecting anything from me, then that must be true. Maybe I should just be grateful for another chance to be with her, even if it was just for two nights. I thought that might be that as well, but now, I realize that's not enough. It's not nearly enough. I want the whole thing, everything. I want what I lost. No. What I threw away. I want it back.

But it's selfish to grab it, even though that's what I want to do. I want to wrap my arms around her and just kiss her until she changes her mind. The same words that Maddie just told me.

I smile at her, feeling a sudden onslaught of sympathy. Maybe she's really fallen for me. With women like that, you never know. She might like me because I'm the big thing right now, or she may truly have feelings for me. A good man will always assume the second one, so I do as well.

I put my hand on her shoulder, and her eyes light up.

"Maddie," I tell her. "You are such a beautiful girl. You can have any guy you point your finger at. Trust me. I know. I was one of them. We'd die to get a single second of your time. Just... look around and find the man who will treat you the way you deserve to be treated."

I don't know if that does the trick or not, but I see the way she's looking at me. She seems incredulous at first, because she wasn't expecting that. She was probably expecting some more banter, where she throws herself at me, and I keep telling her no politely, but in the end, in her mind, we end up together. That's probably been her plan all along.

But I never wanted to string her along. Her, or any other girl, for that matter. I kept telling her that she shouldn't expect anything from me. She agreed. And now, we're here. I guess I'm just like her in my nonexistent relationship with Elsie. I'm running after something that can never be, refusing to accept defeat. In a way, Maddie and I are the same.

"Those are very sweet words," she says, and for the first time, she smiles in a natural way, not in a way that shows you she's trying to flirt or anything like that. She is just being her smiling self, and she is absolutely beaming.

"I think you need to hear them more often," I smile. "Or just keep reminding yourself of them. It should work both ways."

"You're right," she nods. "Do you think..." she starts but doesn't finish her thought.

"Do I think what?" I wonder.

"Do you think I could kiss you, just one more time? For old times' sake?"

I don't say anything to that. Probably not a good idea, if I'm trying to end things. But something is telling me that maybe, she really just needs some kind of closure, and this kiss would be it.

I suck at closure. That much is obvious. Elsie never got hers, and I ended up breaking her heart. I will never forgive myself for that. She probably won't ever forgive me, and I don't deserve to be forgiven. But I can finally understand the need for closure, for rounding things up, so you can mark something as finished, and finally start something else, in a healthy and productive way.

"Just one kiss?" I ask.

"Just one," she agrees.

"Right now?" I ask again.

"What time better than now?" she chuckles.

I guess she's right. Maybe it's best I just get it over with.

Before I can say anything to that, she presses her lips to mine, and there's absolutely no reaction on my part. I just can't force myself. I'm just standing there, numb, like a statue, allowing myself to be kissed.

It seems like a small eternity, when she finally pulls away, leaving my lips wet.

"How was that?" she grins.

Just as I'm about to say something, I notice there's someone behind her, someone who's been watching us the whole time.

"Elsie..." I call out to her, my voice deep, as if I were stuck in some cave, unable to get out.

She doesn't say anything. She looks at me incredulous, as if she can't believe what she just saw. Maddie looks at me, then turns around, and sees Elsie as well. None of us speaks.

Elsie then turns around on her heel and walks away.

I want to run after her, but Maddie pulls me by the elbow.

"Don't," she tells me. "She's not for you. I am."

"I thought you wanted closure," I snarl. "This is all your fault."

I pull my arm forcefully from her grip, and I start running after Elsie. I catch up with her quickly, rushing ahead of her and forcing her to stop and talk to me. Her eyes are wide with shock and disbelief. I don't think I could have made a bigger mistake now than kissing Maddie like that. A fucking idiot. That's what I am.

"Please, stop," I tell her, urging.

"Why?" she asks, shrugging, pretending that this doesn't bother her at all, but I can see through all that. And I won't pretend that it's for the best to allow her to pretend.

"Because I want to explain what happened," I say.

"Why do you think I care to know?" she snorts indifferently.

"Because..." I start, but honestly, why would she want to know?

I haven't earned her trust. I haven't done anything to prove to her that I'm a changed man. If anything, it's the opposite of that. I've shown her just now that I'm just another jock, no better than the rest of them, with the same things in mind. But I'm not. That couldn't be further from the truth, only I can see it in the way she's looking at me that she doesn't want to hear any of my explanations.

"Because?" she echoes, bringing me back to the present moment.

"Because I think you deserve to know the truth."

"The truth?" she repeats. "Oh, you mean like you told me the truth when you dumped me, making me feel like I wasn't good enough for you, the big jock, the future football star? You mean that truth?"

I swallow heavily listening to her speak. All she's said is the truth. This past is still there, between us. And I know in order for us to have a future, first we must sort out the past. But I can't do it on my own. She has to want it as well.

"I don't want to hear that truth," she tells me, shaking her head. "Not now. Not ever. So, please... just leave me alone."

With those words, she turns around and storms away. I watch as the wind plays with the hem of her skirt, making it flutter around her long legs. I watch her, unable to take my eyes off her, and I know that I messed up. Maybe even worse than last time. And I doubt there is any fixing this.

Chapter Eleven

E lsie

I storm into my room, slamming the door shut behind me. Up until a moment ago, Rachel was probably enjoying a calm afternoon, reading at the only desk that we have in the room.

"You got some wine lying around?" I ask Rachel without even greeting her first, and she looks at me flabbergasted, pulling her earphones down so she can hear me properly.

"Wine?" she repeats, obviously thinking that she couldn't have heard me properly the first time.

"I'd prefer wine, but I'm accepting any sort of alcohol right now," I say with an incredible desire to punch through a wall with my fist. I don't know where this rage is coming from, but it's sure better than being depressed.

"You? Want booze? On a Tuesday evening?" she sounds even more incredulous now. "I don't know what's gotten into you, but I'm liking it."

She gets up and walks over to her closet, pulling out an unopened bottle of red wine.

"Red?" she asks, showing me what's in her hand.

"Perfect," I nod. "Open it right now, before I break someone's teeth in."

This time, Rachel bursts into loud roaring laughter, and I know why. This isn't me. I doubt she's ever heard me talk this way. But I'm so pissed I don't know what to do with myself.

"I'll pour immediately, before that someone becomes me," she chuckles sweetly, bringing me a glass of wine instantly. She proceeds to pour one for herself, then sits back on the chair at the desk, while I sit down on my bed, leaning against the wall. "You wanna tell me what's going on now?" she urges.

I inhale deeply. "Where do I start?"

"From the beginning?" she suggests.

"The beginning was a long time ago," I tell her. "But I can start from the middle. That's where all this mess started. I thought I was done with him, Rach. I truly did. Then, he walked into my life again, and I let him hurt me again."

"Wait... you're talking about Callum?"

"Yes," I nod. "Who else?"

She leans closer to me, eager to hear my story. I give her a quick recap of how we saw each twice and slept together both times. She interrupts me there.

"Hold on, hold on..." she shakes her head disapprovingly at me. "Girl, you got laid and you didn't report that?"

"I wanted to," I say, pausing to take a sip. I point at the wine. "This is very good, by the way."

"Never mind that," she waves at me dismissively. "Tell me why you've been keeping me in the dark."

She sounds a little offended, so I explain. "I kept rethinking the whole thing in my mind. I didn't want you to tell me that I made a mistake."

"But I was the one who told you to go ahead and sleep with the guy," she reminds me.

"Yes, but..." I hesitate to continue, although I'm kind of sure she already knows what I'm going to say. "You said to do that thinking that I don't feel anything for him anymore. Which is what I've been saying."

"Yes, that's what you've been saying," she echoes my words. "But something tells me that's not so... is it?"

I shake my head, taking another sip.

"Oh, Elsie, Elsie... you silly girl, what have you gotten yourself into?"

She walks over and sits next to me on the bed.

"You're not over him at all, are you?" she asks, and doesn't need a reply to that question. "Ay, ay, ay," she sighs dramatically, and it tones down the gravity of the situation. We both chuckle, as she pats my knee with her free hand.

"I thought it could be just sex with him," I admit. "I really did. I even told him so. You know, I told him that I don't expect anything from him and that he doesn't owe me anything."

"OK, that was after the first time," she notices. "Then, the second time, he came looking for you here, and I told him you were in the library. I knew something was going on. I just knew it. But I figured, you'd tell me."

"I'm really sorry I kept it a secret from you," I apologize again. "I just... wanted to sort it out on my own, in my own head, you know."

"I understand," she nods sympathetically. "We've all been in such situations. I know exactly how that feels like."

I can't possibly imagine Rachel being so head over heels for someone, but I guess there has to be someone special in everyone's life. She's always been so carefree and open about herself, and she told me, without a hint of embarrassment that if she is ever in a relationship again, it would have to be an open relationship. I can't say I understand the need for that, I can understand that we're all different and that's why we crave different things.

"So, you're not mad?" I ask.

"Nah," she shrugs. "Besides, I should have put two and two together when he came looking for you, but I figured he wanted to talk to you because of what you had in the past and maybe to apologize for being such a jerk."

"Yeah, I didn't get an apology yet," I sigh. "I doubt I'll be getting one, to be honest."

"Why?" she wonders.

"Well, I didn't really finish the story yet."

Her eyes widen with curiosity, and she takes another sip of her wine. "I'm listening," she smirks.

"Again, I don't know where to start," I chuckle a little nervously, but I find a place to continue from. "That second time, in the car, was... incredible. I don't know. I guess, I felt exactly like before, and it frightened me a little. I didn't want him to think that I forgot all about how he treated me."

"Of course," she nods, following the story intently.

"So, again, I told him I'm not interested in rekindling anything, but... I said that out loud to convince both him and myself."

"Did it work?"

"Honestly?" I frown. "No."

She chuckles. "At least you're being honest with yourself. That's a sign of someone with a realistic outlook on life and his current situation."

"Thanks for that, Freud," I tease. "Now, as I was saying... I saw my parents and I don't know... I guess, I felt like maybe, things could get better somehow. Maybe if I saw that he's changed, I could forgive him, if he truly tried."

"Has he been trying?"

"Wait until I get to the worst part," I frown again.

"Oh, crap," she grimaces, allowing me to continue.

"I was walking back here, just after I met with my parents, thinking about him, and who do I run into on campus grounds?"

"Seriously?" she gasps.

"Of course," I nod. "You know how Murphy's law functions."

"Bread always lands jelly side down," she nods importantly, and I can't help but chuckle.

"Exactly," I confirm. "When you least want to see someone, then you'll definitely see them. And it would be fine if we just stumbled onto each other, but that wasn't all. I got there just when he was kissing Madison Palmer."

"Weren't they dating or something?" she wonders.

"I don't know exactly," I shrug. "But I know that they were together on and off, or just had a friend with benefits sort of arrangement. I'm not sure about that."

"But everyone knows she's been haunting him for months now," Rachel reminds me.

"Well..." I sigh. "She's finally caught up with him. Kissing like that in broad daylight, in front of everyone, that's gotta mean something."

"I guess," Rachel nods, probably not wanting to rub salt on my wound.

"You know what?" I suddenly jump up, almost spilling my drink, but it remains safely in my glass, so I down it all, just in case, then I slam the glass onto the table next to me. "This was probably the best thing that could have happened."

"It was?" she sounds incredulous, but willing to hear me out, so I continue.

"If I didn't see this, I would probably believe that he's changed. I might be tempted to think that he's once again that guy I knew before, but now I see that's impossible. You can't go back to being who you once were, because too many things have happened. And he's changed, but not for the better. This guy he is now... I don't want him around me. We don't have anything in common, other than a brief moment we shared in the past. Seeing him kiss Madison only solidified this knowledge, and even though it hurts, I'll be alright."

I spit this out all in one go, mostly because I want to convince everyone that it's really true. I want Rachel to believe it, but mostly, I want myself to believe it. Maybe if I say it out loud enough times, I will eventually see it as the truth.

"What did you feel when you saw him kiss her?" she asks.

I hesitate to tell her, but even my hesitation says more than my words ever could.

"It's OK to admit that you were hurt," she says gently. "You were hoping for something that did not happen. It is natural to feel hurt, betrayed, disappointed."

"I told him I didn't expect anything from him," I remind both her and myself. "So, I guess in a way, he didn't really do anything wrong."

"That's probably what he keeps telling himself about this time as well as the last time," she frowns.

"I'll be fine," I smile. "It's just a rough patch. I've lived through worse, and I'll live through this as well."

"Of course, you'll be fine," she echoes my own words. "You don't need such a douchebag who'll only keep proving to you what a douchebag he is." She makes a disgusted grimace and we both chuckle.

"Thanks," I tell her, looking at her gratefully. "For everything, for being there, for just existing."

"That's what best friends are for," she tells me, walking over to me and wrapping her arms around me.

At that moment, someone knocks on the door. Rachel is usually the one answering.

"Yeah?" she shouts.

"Uhm," we both hear from the other side of the door. "Is Elsie there?"

I swallow heavily, recognizing Callum's voice.

I open my mouth, but I make no sound as I whisper to her. "Why is he here?"

Rachel shrugs. She probably knows even less than I do why he'd be here.

I point at myself, then I shake my head, signaling that I don't want her to tell him I'm here. The last thing I want right now is to talk to him.

This one glass of wine has made me so tipsy that I'm not sure whether I'd slap him or kiss him. So, it's better not to risk either of those two things, because whatever I decide, it'll just make things worse.

I need to remove myself from him for a while, to allow this strange feeling to pass, and I'll be fine. I just need time away from him. Nothing else.

"No, she's not," Rachel shouts back again. "Go away."

I almost chuckle out loud at her rudeness. I know she'd probably tell him far worse things than that, but she's actually trying to be nice, for my sake.

"Listen, Rachel," he says, "I just need to talk to her. It's very important."

"So, go and find her," she replies. "I told you, she's not here."

Rachel looks at me, and nods, assuring me that I am safe here, with her, which is exactly how I feel.

"Can I come in?" he asks, and we both turn pale.

Chapter Twelve

Callum

"I just want to explain myself," I continue, feeling stupid that I'm doing this through closed doors, but the last thing I want to do is enter somewhere where I'm not invited. And it doesn't seem like Rachel wants me there at all. I should probably be grateful that she's even talking to me, which I am.

Rachel is Elsie's best friend. Elsie doesn't want to see me, let alone talk to me. I understand that. But maybe if I explain to Rachel what happened, maybe Elsie will listen to her. That is my only hope of reaching out to her. I can't believe that I've been so stupid to let this happen. I know I can't let Elsie push me away, not before I explain everything to her.

"It's not me you need to explain yourself to," she tells me from the inside. I don't like the sound of her voice. It's pushing me away. It's telling me I'm not welcome here, as if I don't already know that, but I stay, even if that means making a fool of myself.

I regret agreeing to what Maddie suggested. I can see now what a stupid idea that was, to do it like that. Of course, that wasn't any closure. How could it be? And how could I have been so stupid? I frown at myself, remembering the look on Elsie's face.

Ever since all of this started with her, I feel like I'm at a loss, and I have no idea where I am. I'm going forward without having resolved the past, and instead of focusing on that, I'm creating an even bigger mess, by kissing another girl. I'm the biggest idiot there is.

"Please," I say. "I'll just take a few minutes of your time."

"You can't come in," she replies quickly. Then, a pause. "I'm... naked. I mean, not dressed."

"I can wait," I tell her, hopeful that she might speak with me even for a single moment.

"Seriously, it's not me you need to talk to," she repeats herself, sounding annoyed.

"Well, I'd gladly talk to Elsie, but she isn't here," I remind her. I realize that I might need to take more serious, even drastic measures. "If you don't let me in, or at least speak to me in front of the door, I'll just wait for her here, until she returns."

Two girls walk past me just as I'm saying this, and although I feel mortified, I'm not moving. One of them whispers something to the other one, and the two giggle, glancing at me. I don't pay any attention. I know I look ridiculous, talking to someone through closed doors, and especially saying all these things.

But I feel if I let go of Elsie this time, I'm afraid that I'll never find my way back to her. I lost her, because of my own stupidity, and now, I have to be wise and learn from my past mistakes. I want to explain, to tell her everything she needs to hear, and to truly mean it this time, but how can I do it, when she won't speak to me?

I hear some commotion inside the room, then the door unlocks and opens only slightly. Rachel peers through. Her black hair is falling over half of her face, but her eyes are as shrewd as a fox's. I don't know much about her, but one thing is obvious. She really cares about Elsie, and that makes me glad, that she managed to find such good friends, while I... I doubt I could count one of my friends among those truly good ones, the kind you could call up in the middle of the night if you needed something and they would be there.

Such friends, such people are a rare find, and I'm only getting to that conclusion now. A part of me feels like I've been blinded by this superficial talk that I've been surrounded by all this time, but in fact, it's all empty and transient. What truly matters is what you usually don't recognize until it's too late, and I'm afraid this is exactly what's happened to me.

"OK, talk," she orders me, her voice pulling me from the haze of my troublesome thoughts. "I can't let you in. I got someone here. So... make it quick."

"Sure," I nod quickly, grateful for the chance. "I don't know what you know about Elsie and me but– "

"Everything," she cuts me off, sounding annoyed. "I know everything. So, if you just want to repeat what I already know, I'm gonna go ahead and stop you right there."

"No, no," I shake my head, both taken aback as well as appreciating her directness. Maybe if we were all direct and honest like Rachel, maybe we wouldn't be in half of the messes we're usually in. "I... I just want you to tell her that I didn't kiss Madison, she kissed me."

"You kissed another girl?" she frowns at me, sending daggers. I guess I deserve that. "Aren't you a keeper." Those daggers are aimed straight at my heart, and they hit the bull's eye. Then, she takes them, and twists them while they're still inside, making an even bigger wound.

"It was... a misunderstanding," I feel more and more confused under her scrutinous gaze.

At this point, I'm wondering whether it's a better idea to tell Rachel all this, because if I came to Elsie with this poor excuse, I'd slap myself in the face if I were her.

I know that I don't have her, but these last two times I saw her made me believe that perhaps, we could start rebuilding what we had. I was stupid and blind, and I couldn't see what was right in front of my nose. I couldn't realize that I could achieve all my dreams with her by my side. I could have had it all, and now I feel like I don't have nearly enough, although there are many people who would kill to be in my shoes right now. I know that. I understand that, and I'm trying to appreciate what I have, but now that I've seen what I've been missing, it's getting more and more difficult to appreciate something that isn't complete, not in the way you want it to be.

I believed I could get her back, only I went about it exactly the wrong way. I can see that now. But how many times can you make a mistake and still expect to be given another chance?

"A misunderstanding?" she repeats my own words, bringing me back from my thoughts and into the present moment.

"Madison asked if we could have... closure, I guess, and just end this stupid game she's been playing. She wanted a kiss, just... a simple kiss. I stupidly agreed."

"Very, very stupidly," she nods.

"I know," I sigh, raking my fingers through my hair nervously. "But I guess what I wanted to tell you was that for me, it wasn't just sex. Something clicked. I don't know if it was like that for her as well, but I was building up the courage to speak to her about what happened before, because I know I was an asshole, and I really regret how I acted."

I expect her to agree with me referring to myself as an asshole. I expect her to even add salt on the wound here, but surprisingly, she doesn't say anything. She just lets me continue. Strangely, it makes me hopeful that maybe, just maybe, I'm making some progress, no matter how small and insignificant it might seem at first.

"That's what I want to tell her," I add, feeling devoid of the right words to convey my message with. "And, if she still doesn't want anything to do with me, I'll understand. I'll leave her alone and won't seek her out anymore. But... I don't want her to think the worst of me."

"You think you don't deserve that?" She lifts her eyebrow at me. This is a trick question. I can recognize those.

"I do," I admit. "I deserve whatever opinion she's formed of me."

With people like Rachel, you have to be honest. She sees right through any games you might be playing. She figures stuff out immediately. Not that I'm playing any games now. I never considered myself a player, and yet, that's exactly what I've become. People started to celebrate me for all the wrong reasons, and that's not who I am. I can't believe I've been blind for so long.

"But hopefully, I'm not the worst guy out there," I add, realizing that my time is up. She's given me the few minutes which she promised, and I'm losing her interest. Never mind. I said what I had to say. If Elsie wants to hear me out, I'll be happy to explain. If not, well... I can't force someone to do anything they don't want to do.

Losing her the first time was my own fault, just like it is now, but that first time, I was too stupid to realize what I was doing. Now, I'm not. Now, I know exactly what I'm doing, exactly what I'm losing, and it makes this situation ten times more difficult than before. But I know that I've hurt her, and whatever she chooses to decide is completely up to her.

"You're somewhere in the middle," Rachel tells me. Then adds dismissively. "OK, is that all? There's something I need to get back to, so..."

"Yeah, that's all," I nod. "Will you tell her that?"

"Sure thing," she says, then closes the door without adding anything else.

I feel like there's so much left unsaid, but there's nothing I can do about that right now. There is no audience. And even if there was, I doubt my audience would listen to me.

I linger there for a few moments longer, not really sure why. Rachel isn't the kind of person who would open the door again. I can't expect her to.

I finally turn around and start walking back outside. It's gotten dark a long time ago. There is nowhere else for me to go but home, hoping that tomorrow will be a new day, unlike today.

Chapter Thirteen

E lsie

Rachel presses her head to the door.

"Is he– " I start, but she quickly turns to me and presses her finger to her lips urging me to be quiet.

She waits a few moments longer, then nods at me. "I think he's gone now."

I sigh heavily, walking back to the bed, and sitting on it. I rest my hands in my lap, wondering if I should have just opened the door. But then, I remember what I saw, and I feel like I'm back where I was in my first year with him. I allowed him to do the same thing he's done back then. I even welcomed him into it, and that's what's pissing me off the most.

I should have known better. I should have just continued going along the path that I found myself on, even if it wasn't where I wanted to be. At least, my heart wasn't broken. Now, it seems everything that could have gone worse, has actually gone worse. I feel like I have made so many mistakes in the past several years, and they have led me to the point where I can neither go back and start all over, nor can I continue in the same direction, because it feels all wrong. Being stuck is the worst feeling in the world. I know that now. And that realization is crushing me.

I try to focus on being mad, rather than feeling defeated or miserable by my current life conditions. And with Rachel by my side, it's easy to forget about my troubles, even if it's just for a little while. That's why having a best friend like her is so invaluable.

"Ugh," I growl out loud, unable to get rid of this frustration that I'm feeling. At least he's gone and I don't have to talk to him.

"Well," she comes to me and sits down by my side, "you've heard what he said." Just her presence feels soothing.

"It's the same old shit again," I shrug.

"Not really," she replies. "It's still shit, though."

"Mhm," I nod.

We stay like that, in silence for a few moments. I'm allowing it all to sink in, wondering what to do now, where to go from here. Forgiving him isn't an option. I don't even know where that would lead. Probably to more heartache, and that is the last thing I need right now. I have to focus on myself, on fixing my own life, and the only thing I can do is think about him and how much he's hurt me. Again.

"Are you gonna talk to him?" she asks, as if she doesn't know the answer.

"I don't know," I reply honestly. "I'd like to say I won't, but I might succumb to the temptation." I'm almost certain that I will, although I know that it can't bring any good. But maybe, I could get closure this time, or at least an apology. Not that I'd know what to do with either of those two things, but still. Maybe that's what I'm missing here. It's worth a shot.

"Temptation to sleep with him or to talk to him?" she asks, and I can already hear the disapproving tone, which makes me confused, because it was her who assured me it'll be fine. I should relax. I should let go. Well, this is where letting go got me.

But I don't say any of this out loud, because I know that I've unintentionally lied to her. I told her I'm over him, when I clearly wasn't. And that's all on me.

"To talk to him, don't worry," I smile. "I've made the mistake of sleeping with him twice already."

"You know what they say, third time's the charm," she chuckles.

"Not this time," I reply, still smiling. I can only hope that it's a promise I can keep this time. "I managed to delude myself into thinking that I was over him, when I clearly wasn't. And now I'm back to square one. I guess I deserve this, for being stupid."

"No," Rachel shakes her head at me sympathetically. "You weren't stupid."

"What would you call it then?" I tease.

She shrugs. "Gullible?"

"Sure," I chuckle. "That works fine. I'm just afraid that, like the previous time, I might need that closure, you know, for my own sake."

"Then talk to him," she urges me. "If that's what you need."

"You said to sleep with him, and look where that got me," I remind her, but there is no ill will behind that.

No matter how much I'd like to make it sound like all this is none of my fault, but I can't. I did everything on my own, even though I was fully aware that I wasn't ready for this. I wasn't ready to see him again, but I was hoping that one or two nights of mindless sex wouldn't mean anything. I've seen Rachel do it countless times. But I guess that's because she's never done it with an ex. With her, they're always someone next, someone new. She is never going back. Maybe I should learn a thing or two from her. I really should.

She opens her mouth to say something, but I interrupt her. "I know none of this is your fault," I tell her. "I'm just joking. I don't know how else to deal with this."

"It's OK," she tells me, wrapping her arm around my neck, and throwing it over my opposite shoulder. I lean my head onto her shoulder. "If you need to talk to him, talk. If you need to ghost him, then ghost him. This is all about you, El. Not about that douchebag with pretty hair and a sixpack to die for."

"Thanks for reminding me of his best traits," I laugh, pouting playfully at her.

"You know I'm honest," she shrugs, joining in. "Give yourself a few days. Ignore his messages, don't pick up if he calls. Just keep away from him. Then, see how you feel and act accordingly."

That definitely sounds like good advice. Only I'm not sure I can remain so cold and detached if I see his message or notice him calling. I can't pretend that I don't care, when I do. Obviously. But again, it's worth a shot, seeing I have no idea what else to do.

"Yes," I nod, feeling empowered somehow. "That is exactly what I am going to do." I stand up and take my book from the table. "And just to prove that he can't occupy my entire mind, because I won't let him, I'm going to relax now, and read the book I started a few days ago."

"Atta girl," Rachel smiles.

Fifteen minutes later, we're both lying on our own beds. I'm reading my book, and she's with her phone. I'm finding it difficult to focus, but I manage a few pages, when I lift my gaze at Rachel and realize she's staring at me.

"What is it?" I ask. "Do I have something on my face?" I try a joke, but that doesn't lighten the mood. She's still serious. She looks down at her phone, then back at me, still not saying a word. "Come on, what did you find?" I urge. "I'm desperate for something funny. Hopefully, hilarious."

She doesn't say anything at first. It's like she's considering whether to mention anything at all. But it's too late now to go back on whatever that something was. My curiosity has peaked and I'm hoping for some juicy gossip.

"Well..." she says, her voice trailing off.

"What is it?" I ask, a little apprehensively this time.

"You might want to come and see for yourself," she tells me.

I drop my book on the bed, and rush over to her. She shows me her phone, and I immediately stare at the screen. I can see Madison Palmer's Facebook page. I'm not really sure what exactly I'm supposed to be looking at, so look at comments, wall, photos, and a few moments later, I see it. Her relationship status. It says in a relationship with Callum Holland.

I grind my teeth immediately, then quickly remind myself that I shouldn't care about this. We're not dating. We only fucked. Yes, fucked, because that's all it was... obviously. That was what it should have been for me as well. That's how I went, head on, into all this, and now it seems I landed straight on my ass.

"So?" I shrug, trying to look unaffected, but I should have known better than to hide my feelings from Rachel.

"So?" she echoes my own words back to me, with a slight tilt of her head. "Don't even try to tell me you don't care."

"Fine, I won't," I pout. "But that makes no difference to anyone. They're obviously together."

"Didn't you hear what he said through the closed doors?" she reminds me, although I don't really need to be reminded, because I've memorized his every word, and I will probably never forget it.

"I think he's made it pretty clear that he's not to be trusted," I frown.

"I'm not so sure," she says, surprising me. "Madison Palmer isn't the most trustworthy person either."

"That's great then," I announce. "Because that means they deserve each other, and he can leave me the hell alone."

"Is that really what you want?" she dares me. "This is just the two of us here. You can be honest with me. But if you can't be honest with yourself, then you've got a big problem."

I inhale deeply, getting up and walking over to the window. I open it, allowing some fresh air inside, hoping it might clear the mess inside my head, but it does no such thing. The only way I can clear this mess is to speak to him and tell him we're done. To emphasize this. To tell him I don't care about his explanations or apologies, because they serve no purpose. I shouldn't care about them, and yet... I know I do. Once again, I'm doing what I've always done to myself. Lying. And lying has gotten me here.

"I don't know what I expected, but it wasn't this," I start here, as I turn to face Rachel.

"That's good," she nods softly. "It's OK to have expectations. Nothing wrong with that."

"Yeah, but not from the wrong people."

"Ah well…" she says, clicking her tongue against her upper teeth knowledgeably and in an amused way. "You can't know who's wrong or who's right until it's too late."

"Way too late," I add, chuckling.

"Yeah, that one," she nods, joining in. "Just remember not to be too hard on yourself. You allowed yourself to be led by emotions this time. That's OK. It's not your fault."

"I told him I wasn't expecting anything from him," I say again.

"In that case, I guess it's no one's fault," she shrugs. "He took your word for it. Guys aren't mind readers, you know. They can't know when you really mean something, and when you say one thing, but mean exactly the opposite."

"Yeah, you're right," I agree.

Rachel logic has always been infallible. Sometimes, it's difficult to accept, but it always makes sense. And once you come to terms with it, it actually offers some sort of solace.

"As for Madison here," she gestures at her phone, "she can have him. You'll find someone better."

"Of course, I will," I agree, although I'm not all that sure of this yet.

I always believed there was someone out there for everyone. You find that someone, you just click. Now, I'm scared, because that's how I clicked with Callum, but it turned out he wasn't the one for me.

"Listen, I think I have some more wine hidden somewhere," Rachel tells me, jumping up. "How about we pop another bottle open and drink to the death and destruction of all liars and cheats in the world?"

I laugh aloud at her words, as if that might solve anything. But I accept. And for a few precious moments longer, I believe that things could truly get better soon.

Chapter Fourteen

Callum

"Ya'll ready for the big game?"

I hear someone in the locker room ask, and I immediately recognize the sound of that voice. Hunter, the right guard, also the one to keep tabs on how many girls he can sleep with in a single week, roars around us.

I'm seated on a bench, with Jerry and Finch next to me. Jerry immediately replies.

"They know they're getting their asses kicked!" he shouts.

Most of the time, I'm also the one to join in and roar back, but not now. I listen to the hustle and bustle around, feeling somehow... inadequate.

"Yo Call!" I hear my name being called out. "I can't hear you!"

I lift my head at Hunter. He's standing in front of me, fresh out of the shower, with his towel wrapped around his lower torso. There are several tattoos on his stomach and upper arms, and from what he keeps telling us, the ladies love them.

"You ain't gonna wuss out on us now, are you?" he asks, and there's an explosion of laughter following his words.

I know he doesn't mean anything by it. It's just how guy talk in the locker room is. Everyone is a pussy when they don't show enough enthusiasm about a game. Everyone is also a pussy when they do show too much enthusiasm about a single girl. I guess I wasn't paying too much attention to that before, but now, it feels like it's all I can notice.

"Of course not," I say, though I think they can tell I'm not really focused right now.

"Don't fuck around, man," he warns me. "You know that the scouts will be there. And all eyes will be on you."

"That's not true," I shake my head.

Well, partly. The scouts do come when they're very interested in a player, but they do pay attention to the other players as well.

"You know it is," he corrects me. "This could be your big chance, the opportunity you've been waiting for."

I nod, not really saying anything to that. Although, he's right. This is the moment I've been working for all this time. I've been getting better at what I do, so I could eventually be noticed and start playing with the big boys. But somehow, I can't seem to focus on it, not like I used to. I feel like my mind is a mess, and I can't set my priorities straight. Not with the way everything is now.

"The coach will probably talk to you about your priorities," Hunter reminds me, and once again, everyone bursts into a loud chuckle. I feel like he's almost able to read my mind.

I raise my gaze to meet his. He's grinning. So, I grin back.

"I'll show them what I'm made of," I assure him.

He walks over to me and pats me on the shoulder. "I heard you're dating Madison now."

I frown. "From whom?" I ask.

He shrugs as if that doesn't matter. In a way, it doesn't. The only thing that matters is the message, which in this case couldn't be more wrong. Dating Madison Palmer is the last thing on my mind right now.

"I saw it on Facebook," I hear from somewhere behind me, recognizing Tim's voice. I don't turn around to check whether that's true, because Hunter points at him and nods.

"Yeah, that's where," he confirms. "It's her relationship status or something."

I frown again. That's the last thing I need right now, as if don't already have enough on my plate without her jealousy stalking me.

"That's a hot piece of ass right there," Hunter nods, bringing the tips of his fingers to his lips then kissing them, like a freakin' Italian. Again, an explosion of laughter. It seems I'm the only one who doesn't find it all that funny.

"If only I could hit that, only once," another voice joins in, followed by laughter.

Everyone is having a great time. And this is where it hits me. This is what all our conversations look like in the locker room. We talk about the big game that was, the big game that is yet to come, and the girls we either fucked or want to fuck. This is where the list ends.

I listen to them as they continue to talk about Madison and her friends, and who would do who. Quickly, I lose interest, but Hunter drags me back into the conversation. Reluctantly, I allow him.

"Sorry, that's your girlfriend now," Hunter corrects himself. "We shouldn't talk about her like that. At least, not until you dump her for someone else." A few more chuckles are heard.

"I'm not dating her," I say, getting up, and putting on my sweatshirt.

"That's not what she thinks," Hunter replies. "Maybe you oughta straighten it out with her. And let us know as well, if she's available or not."

"She's available," I assure him.

"I think she's got the hots for old Cal," Jerry joins in the conversation. "And you know when a girl is hot for you, she doesn't get cold that easily."

A few whistles fill the room, then Hunter continues with the last girl he fucked, thinking she would be just a one-night stand, but she ended up being some psycho who followed him everywhere he went, calling him up in the middle of the night and harassing everyone he knew. Eventually, she gave up, after a whole year of torturing him like this. I bet he didn't think it was this much fun back then. But everything loses weight after some time has passed.

More stories about psycho ex-girlfriends follow, but I'm not listening. I'm packing up my duffle bag and waving the guys goodbye.

"You up for a party tonight?" Hunter asks before I head out the door. "We have to celebrate our last victory."

"We already celebrated it," I frown.

Hunter seems taken aback by me pointing this out. "Then, we'll celebrate it again!"

He raises his hands up into the air, with a loud woo-hoo sound, which everyone follows and joins in, whistling, laughing, cheering him on. I realize once again that this is all they do. This is who they are. There is no substance in this life. There is no depth. They live for the victory, for celebrating, for getting drunk and for fucking.

I had fun for a while, but it's been getting old. I haven't even been aware of this, until I stumbled onto Elsie again. Our relationship was filled with special moments. Our conversations actually had depth and meaning. We were discussing the future, not just the present moment. And our present moments weren't all about instant gratification. They were about so much more.

I guess I forgot about all that. I got entangled in the flashiness of this life I'm leading now. And I see that if I do obtain my goal, it will be only more flashiness. It makes me question everything I've done until now. I still want to play in the pros, but I'm wondering if it's all worth it. What if the people are just like the people surrounding me now? What if my life stays on this path, and it just becomes worse and worse, despite the fact that I managed to obtain my life goal?

And what after that? What happens when you obtain your life goal?

Isn't the point of that life to share it with someone? I can't imagine spending my life with someone like Madison. I can't imagine spending my life like these guys.

I look at them again. They've already gone back to the same conversation we had over and over again. It's always a question of who fucked who, who had who, who's the worse bitch, who's the toughest guy, who's the one with the biggest black book of names.

I watch them laugh about all these things, and I'm disgusted. I can't imagine ever taking part in these conversations. I can't imagine being one of them. It's not who I am. It's not who I ever was. And it sure as hell isn't who I want to be.

I don't think they even notice that I'm gone. I close the door behind me, heading back to the apartment. On the way there, I grab my phone and call Elsie. I doubt she'll pick up, but I try, nonetheless. It rings a few times, then sends me to voicemail. I consider sending her a message. But I change my mind immediately. If she hasn't replied to my last two messages, I doubt she'll reply to my third message.

But I can't just let it go. Immediately, I turn around and change directions, heading instead towards the girls' dorm. I enter, as it's still early in the evening, and the door locks at 10 pm. Visitors are still allowed. I climb the stairs, walking straight to her room, hoping to find her there.

I knock on the door. I hear commotion inside. My heart is in my throat, then instantly, it slides down all the way to my heels. I feel like running away. But I'm frozen in place. I want to be here, and yet, something is telling me I'm still not wanted here.

The door opens, and the disappointment is evident on my face.

"Oh, it's you," Rachel sniffs at me.

"Yeah, hi," I say, a little nervously, trying a smile, but it's a weak effort. "Is uhm, Elsie here?"

Her brows knit. "No."

Something is assuring me she might not be telling the truth. But I can't very well push her aside and barge into her room, demanding to see Elsie. Although that's exactly what I want to do. I want to grab her in my arms and just kiss her until we both forget about everything apart from the one thing that matters.

Which is?

A little voice asks me this, and I'm not sure if I can still answer this question. The life I've known so far is not what I want anymore. And I can't help but think that Elsie's got something to do with it. In her absence, I was able to convince myself that I wanted all these superficial things, but one look at her, reminded me of the man I was with her. Not the man who dumped her, because the change had already begun there. But the man I was with her, while I was holding her hand, and everything was alright with the world.

I want to tell her all this, and yet, I can't. I'm not allowed to.

"Can you just tell her then that I was looking for her?" I ask, hopeless.

"Sure," Rachel shrugs, and she's about to close the door, when I put my hand on it, preventing her from doing it.

"Please," I tell her. "She's not returning my messages or my phone calls."

That doesn't seem to convince her at all. "I'm guessing if she wanted to, she would have gotten back to you."

I can understand where all this hostility is coming from, and I'm not blaming her. I'm not blaming either of them, but I just need a moment of her time.

"You're right," I nod, pulling back my hand. "I just want to apologize. Nothing else. And apologizing over the phone just isn't right."

At that moment, she gives me a meaningful glance. I don't know how or why, but something happened. Something I said made her change her mind.

"I'll let her know," she says, with a changed tone of voice.

"That's all I'm asking," I smile gratefully.

"But don't get your hopes up," she advises. For some reason, I appreciate it, although we're obviously not on the same side here. Still, I feel like maybe, I'm one step closer to that apology.

"If after this she chooses to ignore me, I'll leave her alone," I tell her.

The words surprise even me, but I realize there is no point running after someone who is doing everything they can to keep you at a distance. If I've hurt her so much that she can't spend a moment more in my presence, then... well, that is my own fault, and unfortunately, her pain to deal with.

The thought of causing her pain again makes me so angry with myself, but there is nothing I can do to ease it for her unless she allows me.

"Thanks," I say, taking a step back. She gives me a smile, then closes the door, ending our conversation.

I don't know why, but I'm hopeful. Mostly, because that is all I can be...

Chapter Fifteen

Elsie

When I heard a knock on the door the following morning, the last thing I thought was that this knock was about to change my entire world.

As always, Rachel, our doorman opens, and I can immediately recognize who it is from the way Rachel greets her.

"Mrs. Medina!" Rachel cheers, as my mom opens her arms and welcomes her into a hug. That's just my mom, a hugger. Rachel usually isn't the one for hugs, but she can't say no to my mom.

"Mom," I walk up to them, allowing them a moment, when my mom releases Rachel from her grip and turns to me. "I wasn't expecting you today."

The very moment I look into her eyes, I know something's wrong.

"Mom?" I ask immediately.

She swallows heavily, her lips parting, as if she's finding it difficult to find the right words to say whatever she came here to say.

Rachel gets the hint instantly. "Why don't I give you guys some privacy, so you can talk in peace?"

I'm stunned into silence, but my mom manages to thank her.

"Thank you, Rachel." Her voice is soft, but there is an undertone of something ominous, something dark.

Rachel grabs her phone from the desk and heads out the door, stopping for a moment. "I'll be over in Linda's room, if you need me."

I nod gratefully, then she closes the door behind her, leaving me and my mom alone. She walks over to me, taking me by the hand.

"Why don't we sit down?" she suggests, and this is how I know that whatever she is about to tell me isn't just bad, it's downright frightful.

I do as she bids, and we both take a seat on my bed. She is still holding me by the hand. Hers is not warm and soft, as usual, but rather clammy and moist. She pats my hand with hers a little, and I can see how nervous she is, which is making me even more apprehensive.

"What is it, mom?" I urge her, although I'd rather just sit here in silence for the rest of the day. But I know we can't do that. She has come to tell me something important, something that obviously couldn't wait for next time when we arranged to meet.

She inhales deeply, looking at me straight in the eyes, her own mirroring mine. She is smiling, but it is a painful smile, hiding so much anguish it makes me want to cry. I blink the need to cry away, focusing on her beautiful face.

"I have something to tell you, my sweet girl," she starts, her voice trembling and on the verge of breaking. "And when I do, I need you to be brave. Can you do that for me?"

The tone of her voice is angelic. It reminds me of the days when I was a little girl, and she would sing me to sleep. It was the sound of that voice that kept me safe through the night, through the worst of darkness, when I would open my eyes and I could only see shadows in my room. All I needed to do was close my eyes and remember the sound of her voice. It always guided me to the morning light.

Only now, I feel like she is the one who needs guidance, not me. And it breaks me to see her so weak.

I swallow heavily, wondering what she could be talking about.

I nod, squeezing her hand. "I can be brave," I tell her, my entire body trembling with fear. "What is it?"

"I suppose there is no other way to go about this, but just say it quickly, like peeling off a bandaid," she says, smiling nervously. "It's... your father."

"What about dad?" My eyes widen in shock, in disbelief. "Tell me!"

"He's..." she pauses to wet her lips, but it's not that her lips are dry. It's that she needs to buy herself some time, so she doesn't start crying, so she can continue with this conversation until the very end. "Your father is very sick."

"What's wrong with him?" I ask, my voice on the verge of breaking.

"The doctors, they..." she pauses again, and I can tell how difficult it is for her to talk about this. I allow her all the time she needs, although I would rather just grab her by the shoulders and shake all this information out of her. "They think it's colon cancer."

"Cancer..." I say the word aloud, incredulous.

It rings inside my mind, like a threat of something terrible, which I can't even imagine. But this threat is real, tangible even. Otherwise, mom wouldn't be sitting here with me, telling me all this now.

"You know your father," she continues. "He is a brave man, and he didn't want us to tell you."

"What?" I ask. "No," I shake my head at her. "I need to know this. Why would he keep me in the dark about something so important?"

"I told him the same thing," she smiles at me, and a tidal wave of love washes over me. The thought of losing either of them fills me with dread. "I don't think he should keep it a secret from you. His reasoning was that he didn't want you to go through all the chemotherapy with him and all the doctor's appointments. He says that isn't what a young woman should be doing."

"No, he's wrong," I keep shaking my head, unable to stop it. "He's my dad. Whatever is happening, I want to be there."

"I know," she beams at me, and I can see the sadness and pride in her eyes. "I also know you wouldn't forgive either of us is something happened to him, and you were robbed of that time with him."

If something happened to him...

Those words remind me how real the situation is, how terribly possible the outcome which I can't even imagine yet. It is too early. I can't lose my dad. I just can't. The thought of going through life without him is too painful to even consider.

"Do you think something might happen to him?" I ask her, although I'm sure that she's not able to answer that question.

But I need assurances of any kind, even if they are false. I want her to lie straight to my face and tell me that everything is going to be alright, even if it won't. That is what I need right now, otherwise I might break down and start crying, without ever stopping. The pain is too great to handle.

"He is in the hospital right now," she explains. "They are doing some tests, to see what stage the cancer is in. Once the lab results come back, we'll know more."

"I want to go with you to the hospital," I tell her.

"Not this time, pumpkin," she replies.

"Why?" I ask. "I want to be there, for you and for dad."

"I know," she tells me, caressing my cheek. "But try to look at this from your father's perspective. He feels... like he is failing us somehow."

"Failing us?" I exclaim loudly.

"You know him," she continues. "He's always been the provider, the one you and I could rely on no matter what. Now, it is our turn to do the same for him, and to be honest, he is not taking it well. He feels... I don't know, almost guilty that he's sick."

"But that's preposterous," I shake my head incredulously.

"Of course, it is," she nods. "And I know you want to be there for him, just give him a few days to adjust to the news that he gets today or tomorrow, when the tests are done. I had to beg him to let me come here and tell you that he's in the hospital."

I look down at our intertwined fingers. This all feels like a horrible nightmare. I wonder if I close my eyes very tightly, then open them again, will I wake up from this into my boring old life, where my only problem was whether or not I should continue with my studies.

How stupid that all seemed now. How irrelevant. Even my troubles with Callum seem like a distant memory now, completely unimportant in the grand scheme of things. I'm just sorry I needed something like this to kick me in the ass and remind me what truly matters in life.

"Alright," I finally tell her. "I won't come today. But I want to come tomorrow. Are you staying at a hotel?"

"We booked a room at The Garden," she tells me about a lovely little hotel, just a few blocks away from the hospital. "I suppose, if they think the results aren't good, they'll keep your father at the hospital, and I'll just go to the hotel for a quick shower and to grab something to eat, then return to the hospital."

I can't imagine my mom being anywhere else but by my father's side. And she's right. Knowing the way he is, he must feel dreadful, but for the exactly wrong reasons. He should be focusing on getting better, but what he's concentrating on is me and whether a young woman should spend time at the hospital by her ailing father's side.

"Can I come tomorrow?" I ask, hopeful.

Of course, I could just appear there. I know they won't send me away. But I don't want to do that to dad. Seeing him in a hospital bed will probably make me cry. And it will make him feel even worse. That's the last thing I want. Now I know what's happening, and I can prepare myself, although I can't promise that I won't cry. I could never make such a promise.

"I'll talk to your father, OK?" she says with a smile.

"OK," I nod. "I won't come until you say it's OK."

"I know, darling," she says tenderly. "I hope you know it's nothing about you. It's your father. And... being in this position where neither of us is able to help him feels dreadful. Do you know that he tried to keep this a secret even from me?"

I chuckle, and she joins in.

"Yes, that sounds exactly like something dad would do," I nod through my chuckles.

"He tried to give me the same excuse he's giving you," she continues. "That he's doing it so I wouldn't worry."

I shake my head, as if incredulous, but in fact, I think we both expected him to do something like that. Unfortunately for him, neither mom nor I are allowing this.

"Well, whether he wants it or not, he's stuck with us," I say, and it feels good to joke. It allows us to forget the truth, even for a precious few moments. "There is no getting away."

"No," my mom agrees, shaking her head.

Then, all of a sudden, she wraps her arms around me, pulling me close to her, so that our chests are pressed against each other. I can feel her heartbeat, and she can feel mine, just like when I was a baby, and I would sleep on her chest. We remain like that for a while, with neither of us willing to let go.

This is the safest place I have ever known. As a child, when I would get hurt, I would run into my mother's arms, and she would make all the pain go away, with just one kiss and one hug. This time, however, not even the magical power of her motherly embrace can make me forget that life had taken a wrong turn somewhere, and it is up to us now to see where it would lead us.

I try to remember her words. We need to be strong, not only for ourselves, but also for dad, even though he thinks he doesn't need us to be...

Chapter Sixteen

Callum

After class, I head out, hoping to stumble onto Madison. The fact that she's going around, telling everyone we're dating doesn't sit well with me. I was trying to be nice all this time, but sometimes, you just have to be rude with people to get your message across.

A few people pass me by, and I just nod at them, not really interested in making casual small talk, as we usually did. In fact, I'm not sure I'm interested in anything right now, other than setting things straight and seeing where I can go from there.

I think of Elsie and how I screwed her over. Again. Without meaning to.

Then, I remember seeing her dad at the hospital. And I feel even worse. I know what that's like to have a family member with a terminal illness. Although I was only seven, I remember it clearly. And I remember the way it made me feel. It's this heaviness inside of you, and you don't know what to do with it. No one can help you, although they probably feel the same way. But they still can't help you. It's something you have to handle on your own, in your own way.

A loud giggle brings me back to reality, and I look around. This is usually where Madison and her friends hang around. It's the central part of the campus ground, and it's a public law that it's their place. A part of me is glad she's there, because I can tell her what I think of her crossing all those lines. But a different part of me still shies away from confrontation, especially if it's with someone I don't know what to expect from.

I consider whether or not to go over there to her, and before I can make up my mind, she waves at me. I can see the grin on her face, overjoyed to see me.

She rushes over and lunges at me, aiming to wrap her arms around my neck, but just as she's about to do that, I grab her by the wrists and prevent her from doing what she planned. She seems confused. This is what in turn, confuses me. She knows what she's done, and yet, she's playing the fool.

"We need to talk," I tell her as softly as I can, although I'd gladly raise my voice, because she's pissed me off more than I can say.

"Sure," she smiles, batting her eyelashes at me.

I take her to the side, a little away from the rest of her squad, but I know no matter how far away from them we are, they'll still try to overhear our conversation. There's no privacy here anywhere.

"What is it?" she asks all innocent, and it takes all my conscious effort not to get pissed even more.

"You know very well what it is," I tell her, trying to keep calm, but it's a thin line I'm walking right now, with everything that's happened.

"I don't know," she shrugs. "We kissed. Your girlfriend saw it? Is that it?"

I blink heavily several times, still trying to keep my cool.

"Yes," I say. "I mean, no, she's not my girlfriend. But you sure seem to think you are."

"Ah," she says, still smiling, as if she has no idea that if she wants us to be together, she's going about it exactly the wrong way. Not that it would ever be a possibility anyway, but still. "If she's really not your girlfriend, then I'm not ruining anything by saying I am, right?"

"That's not the point," I reply.

"The point is that I want you and I know you want me," she says matter-of-factly, as if it's the most logical thing in the world. "When I see that someone doesn't go after what they want, I help them, just like I'm helping you now."

That actually does make sense. And I wish I had a friend like that who would push me in the right direction, when he or she would see that I'm stuck. But none of these people are my friends. Not really. I realize now that they only see me as their friend because I'm popular and a good player. And actually, that first thing is a direct consequence of the second, which means that there is only one single thing that is making me their friend. If I didn't have that, they wouldn't even give me a second glance. Madison wouldn't either, I'm guessing. But this way, I'm a catch and I'm interesting to catch because I keep refusing her. What a messed-up world I got lost in.

"I don't need your help with anything," I tell her, suddenly becoming unaffected by all this.

She shouldn't have any power over me, and she doesn't. She can say whatever the heck she wants, but that still doesn't make it true. This is what I needed to get into my thick head. The only problem I have with her is my own. I put myself in this situation when I agreed to that stupid kiss that was supposed to be the end of things, while in fact, it only made everything more complicated. But that's my own fault. I can't blame that on Madison. She was doing what she's been doing all along, I was just too blind to see.

"What I do need from you is to leave me alone," I finally tell her. "You can put up all the Facebook statuses and shit, but that still won't make them true."

"It will for your little girlfriend," she reminds me, and I can only now see the venom in her eyes. It was one of those if I can't have you, no one will comments. But I don't care. And she knows it.

"If she believes you and not me, then she's not meant for me at all," I tell her, really believing this.

She doesn't say anything. Finally, I say the words that just make her widen her eyes in disbelief, and we keep it at that.

"We're done," I say, emphasizing every single word of it. "I don't want to repeat it again."

She swallows heavily, and her lips part. I wait for her to say something, but there's nothing. She's stunned into silence by sheer acceptance of her inability to control things any longer.

"Glad we got that out of the way," I add, turning around and walking away from her. The sensation is amazing.

I feel liberated from a burden that's been bugging me for a while. Not really suffocating, but it was annoying enough to keep bothering you on a daily basis. At first, I was flattered. I have to admit that. The guys were all jealous that she was into me that much. But I see now that even this feeling was misplaced. Everything about my life somehow fell out of place, and I can only realize all that now, with Elsie back in my life. With her, everything was so much simpler. I was myself. I wasn't someone others wanted me to be.

I consider calling her again, but quickly change my mind. I know I shouldn't be going to her dorm. I know I shouldn't. Every logical fiber in my being is telling me not to do that. She'll think I'm a stalker. She'll think I'm not normal. Even worse, her best friend will think those same things and she'll advise her to stay away from me. I don't know what's worse. But I still keep heading for her dorm, promising myself that this will be the last time I come looking for her.

The very last time.

Soon, I find myself in front of her room.

You can still change your mind. You can still walk away. That little voice keeps telling me, reminding me that there is another option. But for me, that option doesn't exist. I can't give up on this, even when everything else is telling me to. I know this is the last place where I should be, but there is an invisible force keeping me here.

I lift my hand, and I knock. The sound brings me back to the present moment. It orders me to stay here and focus, because this is the last time I will be standing here. I wait for what seems to be a whole eternity, with my entire life flashing before my eyes. And all I see is Elsie.

The door opens and Rachel immediately rolls her eyes anticlimactically at me.

"You again?" she frowns.

"She's not here, is she?" I ask.

I guess even if Elsie is here, I'll probably still get the same reply. But I try, nonetheless.

"No," she says. "This time, really."

I want to ask about the other times, but it doesn't matter. Something in her voice tells me that this time, she might actually tell me the truth.

"I think she'd want to see you even less now than before," she adds.

For a moment, I wonder what could have happened, then it hits me. I remember meeting her dad at the hospital, and suddenly, all the pieces of the puzzle fall into place.

"It's her dad, isn't it?" I ask.

The look of shock on her face is palpable. "How do you know?"

"I have a knack for being in the wrong place at the wrong time," I give her an honest reply. At this point, asking her where Elsie is seems unnecessary. I already have the answer to that question.

I take a step back, but her voice stops me.

"This is not the right time to talk to her about your... status," she warns me.

"I don't want to talk about anything," I correct her. "I just want to be there for her."

"What if she doesn't want you to be there for her?" she asks again, and that is the question I don't have an answer to.

"Then..." I start, pausing for a moment, "then, I'll do as she wants."

"You're not giving up, are you?" she sighs, leaning against the door.

"No," I shake my head. "I won't be an idiot twice."

This makes her chuckle, something I never thought would happen.

"So, you finally got your head out of your ass?" she wonders, still amused. I nod. "Took you long enough."

"Better late than never, right?" I ask, hoping that I'm right.

"Depends," she corrects me. "Sometimes, it's too late to change anything."

I know that's true. She doesn't even need to explain it.

"I know that," I tell her. "I also know how she feels. My grandad died of cancer."

"Oh," she says, obviously not expecting me to open up like that. But I need her to know why I think I might be the right person to be by her side right now. "I didn't know that. I'm sorry."

"It's OK," I shrug. "I was a little kid. But you never forget something like that. I know that it's different when it's a parent, but my grandad was like a father to me. His death left a big hole in my life..." I rake my fingers through my hair, realizing that I've gone way too deep. She doesn't need to know any of this. Heck, I doubt she even cares. But she's polite enough not to interrupt me. She's actually listening.

"I guess what I'm trying to say is that I understand what she's going through," I add. "I just want her to know that she's not alone."

"Even if she sends you to hell?" she wonders.

"If that's where she wants me to go, that's where I'll go," I nod.

I take another step back, expecting her to say something else, in an effort to stop me from going where I feel I need to go. But she doesn't say anything. She just stays there in the doorway, staring at me, a smile lingering in the corner of her lips. I still have no idea which side she is on. Elsie's, of course. But perhaps she's somewhere in the middle, now that she's seen all I want is to help Elsie.

I lift my hand to wave at her, but I stop somewhere mid-way. I turn around and rush outside. There is only one place I have to be now, and I'm wasting every second that I'm not there.

Chapter Seventeen

Elsie

I'm pacing up and down the hallway, like a caged animal. That is exactly how I feel. Caged by my own fears, the situation, the realization that there is absolutely nothing I can do about this that could make any significant change. Nothing. And it's killing me.

I pass by the door where my mom walked in first, telling me to wait outside. I wanted to push my way in next to her, but I know why she told me to be patient. It's the most difficult thing she can ask of me now. Yet, I do my best to oblige. This isn't any situation that I know. I feel like everything I do or don't do might have catastrophic consequences.

But mostly, I'm scared. Scared and angry. I feel like a little girl, and I just want to cower in some mouse hole and stay there until everything is alright again. Only, the most frightening thing is that there is a possibility that nothing will ever be the same again. I dare not even think about it, but no matter how hard I try to banish that realization, it keeps walking by my side, reminding me of its ugly presence in every waking moment of my life, since mom told me about dad's illness.

I know she will come out any moment, beckoning me to join her inside. I will have to face dad. I never thought that I'd ever say such a phrase. Face dad. I always thought if such a phrase did pop up, that would mean that I did something wrong. But that's not the case. No one did anything wrong, which is what makes this so difficult. There is nothing to apologize for, and yet, I feel like I want to point the finger of blame somewhere, in any direction, as if that will make me feel a little better.

At that moment, mom opens the door, peering outside. I can see the red circles around her eyes. She's been crying. I've only ever seen my mom cry three times, with this being the third time. She cried when grandma died. She cried when she finished watching the movie Life Is Beautiful. And she has been crying now.

She tries to smile at me, but it's a weak effort. Still, I appreciate it.

"Would you like to come in, darling?" she asks, as if she's inviting me somewhere where I truly want to go, while I would gladly run away in the opposite direction and just keep going until I forgot what I was running from.

My lower lip is trembling, and I can barely reply, but there is an audible yes that came from me, followed by a nod. She disappears back into the room. I swallow heavily, looking at the doorway, as if it would take me to a whole new world. In a way, it will. A world I never thought I would be a part of. A world I always thought would never clash with mine.

I muster all of my strength as I step into the room. Immediately, the beeping of machines and the blinding lights of the white walls attack my eyes mercilessly. I blink heavily, as my retinas adjust, and a moment later, what was initially just a shadow in the form of a lying man has now transformed into my father.

It takes all my conscious effort to stifle my gasp. It seems like he's lost weight in the two weeks that I haven't seen him. Looking at him like that, it feels like years had passed. He makes a better effort at a smile than my mom.

"Hey, champ," he calls out to me, adjusting himself in the bed, so he's not lying anymore, but rather sitting upright, propped by a pillow against his back. Everything is so painfully white, even him. It's hard to look at him, at the room. "Come, sit next to me." He pats the space by his side. Even his hand looks a bit dry, his fingers longer than usual.

I do as he tells me. I sit by his side, feeling like a little girl once again, powerless before the world, before life, before reality. Everything came crashing down around me, falling apart in a blink of an eye. I don't feel ready to have this conversation. I don't feel even nearly ready. But

I'm here, and there is nowhere I can run away to. Even if I could run away, this would mean turning my back to my family. I can't do that, no matter how painful it is to stay where I am.

"You do understand why I didn't want you here?" Of all the things he could have started with, he starts with this one. His voice is steady, confident. There is not a hint of doubt in it. If I close my eyes, just listening to him, I might make myself believe that we're not where we are. But my eyes are wide open

I nod, unable to find my voice. I glance at mom. She's standing in the corner, looking at us tenderly. Even from this distance, I can see that her eyes are filled with tears. She will look away at some point, wiping them with her sleeves, thinking she's good at hiding it.

"All this," he gestures around him, as if he were the king showing me his kingdom, "is nothing scary. They just want to make sure that the cancer is treatable, which I've been told it is."

I nod again. I wasn't expecting this conversation to be this difficult. I expected it to be hard, but not like this. I thought I would keep it together. I thought I would be in control of my emotions, but it's exactly the opposite. I feel like I can't allow myself to speak, because if I do, it will all start pouring out of me and I won't be able to stop crying. It's better to be quiet and listen to him.

He lifts his gaze to meet mom's. Then, it's back on me again.

"I know this is very difficult for you," he says, as if reading my mind. I guess that shouldn't come as a surprise. "That's why I didn't want to tell you any of this. You shouldn't be worried about me. You should be worried about your own life." He suddenly pauses, then slaps himself on the forehead, laughing. "Wrong word. I didn't mean worry about your own life. I mean, focus on your own life. Because I know there is nothing worrisome about you. You have always been a wonderful daughter, so confident and conscious of her own choices."

Right now, that is the worst thing he can tell me. I can't handle it anymore, as my eyelids press together heavily, and an onslaught of tears starts streaming down my face.

"Hey, hey," he leans over to me, wiping the tears from my cheeks. "No crying, come on."

He cups my chin with his fingers and makes me face him. "I'll be fine," he tells me, and I want to believe him with every fiber of my being. The alternative is unimaginable. "This is just a minor hiccup. Nothing to worry your pretty little head about."

I nod again, managing to smile. I feel guilty. I should be the one making him feel better, and not have it the other way around. My dad will always be my dad, and I know that no matter what happens, he will always want to be the protector, the one to provide shelter and comfort to me and mom. He has just proven me right on this one.

But that doesn't mean that I don't want him to know that both me and mom can be strong, when he needs us to be. I need to show him this, just like he's shown me how brave and strong he is. The thought almost creates another onslaught of tears, but I manage to fight them off. I'll cry in front of mom, when he can't see.

As always, mom jumps to the rescue.

"Sweetie, why don't you go and get us two coffees from the machine?" she suggests softly. "There's one just down the hallway. Or you could go to the cafeteria and get us two cappuccinos. They're not amazing, but it's better than the coffee sweat the machine makes."

Dad chuckles at the coffee sweat joke, and for a moment, it almost feels like we're not in a hospital and dad isn't sick. But it just lasts a single moment. One stolen moment in time, which then gets trampled by reality.

"Sure," I get up, realizing that it's not about the coffees at all. It's about giving me a moment to gather my thoughts and have a moment to myself.

This is overwhelming for everyone. Mostly for dad. I feel like I'm making it somehow about me, and that's exactly the wrong reaction. I want him to see that I'm not a weak little girl anymore. He can rely on me. He can count on me, even in times of need.

"I'll go to the cafeteria," I tell mom. I don't ask dad, because mom already mentioned that they're waiting for him to be called for more tests, and he was only allowed a light breakfast and water. Nothing else.

"We'll be here," dad reminds me, winking as he speaks, and I have to admire his courage.

Even at a time like this, he wants to show us that he is not giving up, that he is still the man we always thought him to be, as if afraid that this might change if we see him broken down by illness. The thought grips at me violently, and I want to wrap my arms around him, like mom does, and then not let go for at least five minutes. But I know that right now, it might have the opposite effect. He might think I'm feeling sorry for him. So, I resist the temptation.

It's strange. This illness is making me question my every action, wondering what kind of an effect it might have on my dad, while in fact, I should just act as I think fit, and hug him if I feel like it. But I can't do that.

I get up from the bed, walking over to the door. I pause, feeling the need to say something, anything. But there is a ball of yarn inside my throat, suffocating every sound that I want to make, leaving me gasping for air. This whiteness is asphyxiating. My eyes hurt again, a tidal wave of pain washes over me again, and I push the door open, stumbling outside into the hallway, closing the door behind me.

Breathing heavily, as if every breath were my last one, I head down the hallway towards the coffee machine, but I don't stop there. Tears are clouding my sight. I wipe them quickly, hastening my step, when suddenly, someone calls out my name.

I immediately recognize the voice. Something inside of me clenches. I dare not turn around. A part of me can't believe it's who I think it is. A million questions start swarming inside my mind.

Why is he here? How did he know where to find me? What does he want from me?

I try to keep going, but something makes me stop. No matter what, I can't just turn my back to him. That would make me as bad as he was, and I promised myself I would always try to treat others better than they treated me. With him, this should be quite a test.

I sigh heavily, finally turning around.

"Yes, Callum?"

Chapter Eighteen

Callum

Elsie turns to me with a blank expression on her face. I feel like I'm imposing on her personal space, and in a way, I am. I shouldn't be here, especially not at this moment. But something is telling me that I am exactly where I need to be, at exactly the right moment.

"What are you doing here?" she asks, as I'm still struggling to find my voice.

I know she must think this is all a game to me. I haven't shown her at all that this is as serious for me as it is for her. I'd like to think that it's because I haven't been given the chance to prove myself to her, but the truth is that I've had many chances, all of which I somehow let slip through my fingers, like fine grains of sand.

"Did Rachel tell you I'm here?" she asks again, suspicious that her best friend worked against her best interests in mind.

I assure her that isn't the case. "Don't blame Rachel." She frowns, unconvinced. So, I continue. "She's been telling me to stay away from you every time I came looking for you."

"Why wouldn't you listen?" she voices.

"Because I can be stubborn sometimes," I shrug. It's the truth and she knows it. I like getting my way. I've always been like this. But I also know when I need to stop. Maybe I should have stopped trying to get to her already, but I feel like I owe her so much more than just to disappear from her life again... unless that is what she wants me to do. In that case, I'll do exactly that.

"Can I explain that whole situation with Madison?" I ask, all hopeful.

She sighs, her face scrunching up at me in displeasure. "I don't care about any of that right now. It's totally irrelevant."

"I know," I nod, biting my tongue in an effort to prevent myself from spilling that I knew about her dad even before she did. "Are you headed down?" I ask, gesturing at the elevator.

She looks in the same direction. "Cafeteria."

"Can I walk you there?" I ask.

"If you have to," she says, shrugging, then heads for the elevator and I follow.

She presses the button, and the elevator arrives, taking us down to the ground floor, where we head to the cafeteria together. She orders two cappuccinos, then turns to me.

"Are you having anything?"

"I'll just have an espresso," I nod, taking out my wallet to pay.

"You don't have to pay," she tells me, already putting the money on the counter. Her tone of voice assures me that I won't be able to change her mind. So, I'm considering this one of those lost battles that might help me win the war.

We wait for the coffees, then she puts hers down on a table.

"I need to take these back," she tells me.

I'm trying to read her voice, hopeful for just a small sign that might tell me she's glad to see me here. But there is nothing. All I hear is pain and fear. I know where that's coming from. Everything inside of me wants me to wrap my arms around her and just hug her until she's ready to talk about it. But I wouldn't mind being with her in silence.

I've been listening to so many stupid talks and stories in the past months. I can't believe that I just kept absorbing them into myself, not even realizing that they were dumbing me down. All I could focus on was football. Nothing else. As if there was nothing else in the whole world for me, but football, booze and girls. But all those things grow old fast. I was trying to make them last. I see that now. Pushing the borders, pretending that I was really having fun, but in fact, I was drowning, and because I couldn't see a way out, I just allowed the water to wash over me.

I want her to know that she can trust me. But I can't tell her what I know before revealing that I've known it longer than she did. And that might create an even bigger gap between us, which is exactly the opposite of what I'm trying to achieve.

"Sit down with me for a moment," I urge. My eyes plead with hers. "Please."

She hesitates for a moment, then does as I ask. We both sit down at a table, facing each other. She puts her hands on it, intertwining her fingers. She glances at me, then diverts her gaze.

"I know this is the worst moment for me to ask you to listen," I start. "But I'm afraid that if I let you go now, I might never get a chance to explain." I expect her to say something to that, but she doesn't. So, I continue. "I know you said I should not expect anything from you and believe me that I went into this exactly like that. I was drawn back to you, remembering all the good times we had together."

"Yes, the good times you decided to throw away," she reminds me, although there is no animosity in her voice. It is a soft acceptance of things as they are and as such, cannot be changed.

"I know," I nod. "I also know that no matter how many times I apologize for this, you won't be able to get past what I did. And I understand that. I know I've hurt you too much."

"It just seems that once wasn't enough." This time, there's a bit of venom in there.

"Madison kissed me," I try, but the moment I say it, I realize how weak an explanation that is.

"Poor you," she frowns. "Do you expect sympathy?"

I swallow heavily. This isn't going the way I was hoping it would. Honestly, I have no idea what I expected to happen here. I surely wasn't expecting her to forgive everything and just fall into my arms. The walls she has around her heart now are my own doing. She built them up after I dumped her, after I made her feel like she wasn't good enough for me, while the truth was, I wasn't good enough for her. I can see that now. I can only hope that she sees it, too.

"I don't expect anything," I tell her, shaking my head.

A few people pass us by. They seem to be lost in their own conversation, but I still pause, waiting for them to pass. It buys me a few precious moments to come up with the right words to say.

"I don't expect anything," I repeat, "for the simple reason that I don't deserve anything from you. Even you sitting here is something I'm grateful for, because you chose to give me your time."

She doesn't say anything to that, but I take the silence as something positive.

"I just wanted to say that I hoped this could be the start to something..." I say, realizing that maybe I'm crossing the line, maybe I'm saying more than I should be saying, and that she'll pull away from me before I even have the chance to explain everything.

"Listen," she suddenly interrupts me, looking down at the coffees. "I really can't deal with this right now. It happened and yes, you hurt me, but I don't want to talk about it now. So, I'm sorry, but you came for nothing."

With those words, she stands up, pulling the chair behind her loudly, making it screech against the floor. A few people turn around, curious to see who's making that noise. She doesn't pay any attention to them.

"None of this matters now," she adds, as if she wants to leave, but something's keeping her here.

"I know that your dad isn't well," I say, immediately biting my lip. I didn't want to show her that I knew any of this. I also didn't want Rachel to get in trouble, when she said nothing. It was all me who figured it out. But I don't know what's worse. Letting Elsie think Rachel told me everything or revealing that I knew about her dad's illness before she did?

The moment she hears me say this, her eyes widen.

"Rachel told you everything?" she asks, sounding incredulous.

All I need to do now is nod. Make Rachel take all the blame. That's what all my so-called friends would advise at a moment like this. But those aren't my friends, and that isn't the kind of advice I need. Not if I want Elsie to start trusting me again. There is only one way out of this mess, and that is the truth, no matter what the consequences might be.

"No," I shake my head, inhaling deeply. "Rachel just confirmed what I already knew."

"What did you know?"

This is the moment of truth. I can just be quiet about meeting her dad. I could come up with numerous lies, one better than the other. But I would get entangled in them, and this entanglement will pull us apart. She is here, willing to hear me out. I can't lie to her. Not now. Not ever again.

"I stumbled onto your dad here, at the hospital," I explain slowly, carefully choosing each word. Perhaps if I keep quiet about when it happened, I might soften the blow. But she seems to be able to read my mind. Women sometimes have that ability, without even realizing it. And right now, her sixth sense is spot on.

"When was this?" she demands to know.

"It was... maybe a month ago," I say, realizing that she is about to draw all the conclusions on her own. This is where she either allows me to stay with her or she pushes me away forever.

"You..." she starts speaking, but her voice is on the verge of breaking. Her entire body is trembling, under the influence of what she just realized. "You've known for a whole month that my father is ill?"

There is no rage in her voice. I would be able to handle rage. Anger. Frustration. Any sort of negative emotion. But there is nothing like that. Instead, her voice is laden with sorrow, with disappointment, with disillusionment. And it's all my fault.

No matter what I say to that, whatever words I use, she will keep pulling away from me. I can see it in her eyes, in the way her entire body is rebelling against the thought of accepting the fact that I've known this before her and refused to tell her.

"I'm sorry." My words sound empty, devoid of real depth, but that is solely because I feel like they serve no purpose, other than to fill the silent void that has been created between us.

Her lower lip trembles. I want her to shout at me, to slap me, to push me away, to do something, anything that shows me that I still exist to her. But she does nothing. She is merely staring at me, as if she's seeing nothing, and that is what hurts the most. I provoked no reaction inside of her. I don't exist to her anymore. And that is what hurts the most.

She grabs the two cups of coffee and turns to go, when I try to grab her gently by the elbow, to prevent her from leaving she sears me with her gaze, her lips pressed together, as if purposely preventing herself from saying a single word to me. I understand. I understand everything, but that still doesn't mean that I can't be sorry for everything I've caused.

"I'm sorry," I repeat.

The words dissipate around us, as if they were never said. They might as well, because I know she didn't hear them. The wall is too high for anything to reach her.

She looks down at her elbow, caged by the bars of my fingers. She doesn't say anything. She doesn't have to.

I release the grip I had on her, and without a single word more, she turns around, walking away from me... this time, for good.

Chapter Nineteen

Elsie
I stumble onto mom in front of dad's hospital room, and I can't hide that I'm upset. She takes the coffee from my trembling hand, leading me to sit down on the two chairs that are conveniently placed in front of every room.

Neither of us speaks for a while, and it feels good somehow. I'm not forced to speak. The truth is, I feel like there is so much to say that I wouldn't know where to start. People walk past us hurriedly. Nurses, doctors, visitors, like us. Life just keeps on going, no matter how much you'd like it to stop, to focus on the present moment and try to see what you can do about the future. The future that I see before me is uncertain, frightful even.

"This coffee isn't half bad." I hear my mom's voice.

I turn to her. She's smiling at me. But the deep, dark bags underneath her eyes tell a different story.

I don't feel like eating or drinking anything right now, but I take a sip, more for my mom's sake than mine. She watches me do it.

"How are you holding up?" she asks.

I shrug. I wouldn't know where to start explaining why I feel the way I feel.

"You don't have to stay here all the time with us, you know," she tells me tenderly. "We know you have your classes and well, your life."

"You are my life," I remind her.

She smiles even wider this time, and suddenly, her entire face lights up, almost as if everything's alright, and we're not at the hospital, but some other people entirely.

"No," she corrects me. "You are our life. We are just your parents. And we've done our part in raising you into this wonderful young woman that you are today. But your life is just starting. Of course, we are still a part of it, but a minor part, and that is exactly how things should be."

"You can't expect me to just go back to my dorm and pretend like none of this is happening," I frown, putting my coffee cup down on the floor, between my feet.

"That's not what I am saying at all," she continues. "I am simply saying that you shouldn't feel obliged to spend days and nights here. You can just come in the afternoons, for an hour or so."

I know what she is trying to do. She is trying to keep me on the sidelines, so I don't have to watch the difficult parts. I appreciate her efforts at protecting me as always, but I can't imagine not being by my dad's side, even if things turn for the worse.

"If I'm not here, and something happens to dad, I..." I finally dare to tell her my deepest fear, but my voice betrays me, and I'm unable to continue.

She turns to me, and wraps her arms around me, as she's always done. I inhale her familiar scent, allowing it to enshroud me in a feeling of safety, as if nothing could ever harm me while she's got her arms around me. We remain like that for a while, breathing in, then exhaling slowly. I manage to calm down, and once she senses this, she lets go of me.

"You know," she suddenly starts, and from the tone of her voice, I realize she's trying to steer the conversation to a different direction, just something to distract us both with. "I thought I saw someone familiar a bit earlier, while I was back down at the reception, handling some paperwork for your father."

"Who?" I ask, not even dreaming that I would hear the answer she gives me.

"That guy you used to date," she says a bit distractedly, gesturing with her hands as she always did, as if moving her hands left and right helped her remember someone's name. "You know, in your first year. The football player?"

I feel like she punched me in the stomach with those words.

"You saw him, too?" she immediately adds, and I know she's read everything on my face.

"Yes," I nod, not seeing a point in lying to her. "I stumbled into him at the cafeteria. He, uhm... he had some injury and was here for a checkup." I come up with a white lie quickly, not because I don't want to share this with her, but because now is not the time to be focusing on my love life, when my dad is lying in the hospital, waiting for results.

"You know, I always liked him," she says, absent-mindedly.

I haven't really told my parents exactly what happened with him. The version I gave them was that it was a mutual break up, which we both agreed on.

She sighs, continuing. "I wish you could find someone who would treat you the way a girl like you deserves to be treated," she tells me with a smile. I don't like this topic, because I know she's talking about this just so that we don't focus on what's been eating us up alive. So, I entertain her.

"I'm focused on my studies now, mom," I remind her, feeling a pang of guilt at these words. "Guys aren't really my priority now."

"And they shouldn't be," she nods. "Just... it's nice to have someone you can rely on, especially in situations like this."

"I can rely on you," I say.

She lifts her gaze to meet mine. There is so much love in it, so much compassion and so much pain.

"Of course, you can, darling," she confirms. "I'm just saying that we might not be– "

"Excuse me, Mrs. Medina?" A voice interrupts her, and we both look up, seeing a doctor, who's holding a bunch of papers in his hand.

"Yes," mom nods.

"I would like to speak to you regarding your husband's results," he continues, looking at me.

"Of course," she nods again, standing up. I immediately do the same.

The doctor is the first one to enter dad's room, then mom, then me. I don't even consider the option of staying outside. Mom walks over to dad, taking him by the hand. I hesitate, but then, he smiles at me, reaching for me with his other hand. Once again, it takes all my conscious effort not to allow a stray tear to roll down my face. I can't have that happen. Not now. Dad needs me, and this is the moment where I have to show him that I'm strong enough to handle this.

We all stay like that, holding hands, our eyes fixated on the doctor. He's a middle-aged man, with thick-rimmed glasses and a kind-looking face. His voice is steady, comforting even. I'm sure it comes in handy in his line of work.

"I have the sigmoidoscopy tests... abnormality... colon cancer... stage II..."

The words he's bombarding us with feel like an onslaught, and all I want to do is press my hands to my ears like a little child, and pretend that I didn't hear any of it, because if I didn't hear it, it means it's not true, it's not happening. But I'm not a child anymore. I am a grownup, a grownup who is facing the ordeal of a lifetime, and no matter how much I try to close myself off from it, it won't make it go away.

"From the results that we have," the doctor continues, as no one else is talking or asking any questions, "it seems that the cancer has grown through the wall of the colon, perhaps somewhat into the nearby tissue, but we are almost positive that it hasn't spread to the lymph nodes, which is a good sign." He pauses for a few moments, allowing that information to sink in. "The patient will need surgery, in order for us to remove the section of the colon containing the cancer along with nearby lymph nodes. It's called a partial colectomy and from what we believe, we should be able to clear the threat."

"Well, that's very good news indeed," dad breaks the ice, and we all smile.

"We shall run some more tests, however," the doctor adds, adjusting his glasses by pushing them up his nose with his middle finger, "just to be on the safe side. If the cancer is high grade, that is if it looks... well, more abnormal than usual when checked closely in the lab, or if we see that it has grown into nearby blood or lymph vessels, in that case, we may need adjuvant chemotherapy, which is chemotherapy after surgery, as in such cases, there is a risk of a recurring cancer."

He looks at dad, expecting another response, but dad just nods this time.

"Whatever you need to do, doc," dad finally tells him, squeezing my hand. He sounds so strong, so confident, but I can feel how clammy his hand has gotten. I don't think I've ever felt his hand so moist. "I need to get better, because if I don't, who's gonna take care of my girls?"

That is the moment when I break down. Tears just start streaming down my face. I'm not even trying to stop them. I'm controlling my breathing, so I don't burst into sobs, but that is as much as I can do.

The doctor notices immediately, giving me an awkward smile. "The prognosis is very optimistic," he tells me, then takes a step back, heading for the door. "I'll give you a moment, then I'll send the nurse to take you for some additional tests."

He almost tiptoes out of the room, closing the door behind him, and as if I were waiting for that very moment, a loud sob explodes from somewhere deep inside of me.

"I'm sorry," I say, sitting down on the bed, next to dad, and wiping my nose with my sleeve. I don't care about propriety and such stupid things at a moment like this.

Tears are muddying my sight. I try to clear it up by blinking heavily several times, but it only makes me cry even more. Mom walks around the bed and comes to my side, standing behind me. I feel her hands on my shoulders. Their presence and love are all around me. I feel blessed to have them, but that thought only brings me more pain, because I might lose dad. No matter how optimistic the doctor is, the danger is always there, it never leaves my mind. It is a cruel possibility, that I might continue my life without him.

Who's gonna take care of my girls?

His words echo inside my mind, mocking me.

"It'll be fine, muffin," dad tells me softly. "You heard the good doc. He knows what he's saying."

I nod, sniveling.

"Just look at it as some routine operation," he continues. The more I hear his voice, the more soothed I feel, and I know that's what he wants to achieve. "Like a tonsil removal."

I chuckle at the preposterous comparison. "That's hardly the same, dad."

"It can be if you make it so," he shrugs, grinning. "They'll just snip, snip a little here, a little there, and I'll be home before you know it."

There is nothing else I would like to believe more than this. And just by looking at him, he somehow manages to calm me down. It's a magical skill every loving father has. He knows exactly what to say at exactly the right moment. Heck, he would be able to convince me that black is white, if he wanted to. That's how powerful his convincing skills are.

I inhale deeply, then exhale. I realize that I'm not crying anymore. He achieved his goal.

"There we go," he smiles, as mom squeezes my shoulders tenderly. "Now, why don't you tell us what's going on with you? I'm so tired of constantly being the center of attention here."

Mom giggles sweetly. "Oh, you love it, and you know it."

"You got me," he teases, and we all burst into laughter. "But I really think that it's time we heard what Elsie's been up to."

Their eyes are focused on me. I want to tell them everything, how difficult it's been, how torn I've become regarding my life choices, how afraid I am that I've made too many mistakes and I don't know where to turn to now. But the hope in their eyes is overwhelming. That's not what they want to hear, not now at least. They need me to shift focus onto more pleasant things.

So, I do.

Chapter Twenty

Callum

It's been three days. Three long, endless days of me fighting myself.

I feel like I ruined everything again. And just like the previous time, I have only myself to blame. No one else. Least of all Elsie.

I can't focus on anything, least of all the game we have tomorrow. It's all the other guys are talking about. It's all the whole campus is buzzing about, as if nothing else in the world matters but that one game. They keep asking me if I'm ready, and I give them the only answer there is to give.

Of course, I'm fucking ready.

I've been ready for this my entire life. I feel like the moment has finally arrived, the moment I've been working for all this time. All my efforts have been aimed at this. Everything I've ever given up on, I gave up for this. And yet, I can't even fully focus on it. My dream come true is at an arm's reach, but I feel like it's still too far away for me.

It's still early in the evening, when I leave the locker room, unable to listen to more talk about the upcoming game. I feel torn, guilty that I'm not as excited as everyone else is, so I almost sneak out of there, like a thief in the night, fearing they might see that I don't share their enthusiasm. But it's difficult to be happy and excited about something, when someone you care about deeply is going through the worst time of their lives.

All the lights around the campus are on. There are still many people out, as it's a pleasant, summer night. There are banners everywhere. It seems that everyone's ecstatic about the upcoming game, whether they're playing or not.

Just as I turn around a building, trying to avoid the crowd in the very center, by the big fountain, I bump into someone.

"Umph!" I hear someone grunt, dropping a few books to the ground.

When I take a closer look, I realize it's Rachel.

"Sorry about that," I tell her, as we bend down together, picking up her books. I hand her the one I'm holding and after a moment of hesitation, she takes it. "I didn't see you," I explain.

"It's fine," she says.

I can see that she's not in a good mood, but I can't tell if she's pissed or upset. With some girls, their facial expressions are just like that, unreadable. Although you can easily tell that something's wrong. I immediately think of Elsie.

"How's Elsie?" I ask.

"She's been better," she replies cryptically.

"How's her dad?" I ask, but I have little hope that she'll tell me.

"I don't know if I should be telling you anything," she replies.

"I won't stalk her," I say. "I gave her the space that she needed. I don't want to bother her in any way. I was just wondering about her dad because I know the man."

She seems taken aback by what I said, as if she wasn't expecting it. She looks at me with a tilted head, then takes a step back.

"The operation is tomorrow," she finally tells me.

"The operation?" I echo. I know exactly what she's talking about, but the word just escaped my lips, out of a lack of anything better to say. She only nods. "Tomorrow when?"

"Tomorrow afternoon at six." She pauses, eyeing my reaction. At first, I don't connect the dots. She does it for me, a moment later. "It's exactly when the game starts."

My mind is blank, but the moment she says it, I realize the meaning behind her words. The universe is forcing me to make a choice. It's either to go after my dream or to go and get the girl of my dreams. I can't be in the same place at the same time, which means I can't be there for both of those things.

"Tough choice, huh?" she asks, seeing I got lost in thought.

I blink heavily, as her words reach me one at a time.

"She doesn't want me there," I say, feeling like I'm making excuses.

"She's upset," she shrugs. "Of course, she doesn't want you there. You fucked up. Bad."

"I know," I sigh, my shoulders raising then dropping down quickly as I do so. "Do you think there is hope?"

I have no idea why I'm even asking her this. Not like she's my friend. She's Elsie's friend, her best friend at that. Why would she want to help me? But then, I remember that she did help me by telling me where Elsie was. Maybe I did manage to convince her that I'm not such a bad guy as I seem to be.

"There's always hope," she surprises me with her answer. "It just depends on what you're willing to sacrifice for your ultimate goal."

I always thought I knew what my ultimate goal was. To play in the pro league. That has been my dream all along. I never thought there would be anything I would consider even remotely as important as that. But now I feel like I don't know anymore. I feel like my own aspirations steered me towards my dreams, but everything along the way forced me to change, and now at what could be the end of this journey and the beginning of a new one, I feel like I'm not the same person who started all this. I fell under the influence of those around me, choosing to turn my back to people who truly mattered, who would have supported me no matter what.

I'm questioning everything, even my own goals. Are they truly worth it, if I need to change who I am in order to obtain them? Do I become a sell out for the money and fame, so I could do what I want? Or do I try to do it the other way, staying true to myself and to those who accepted me when I was nobody and had nothing?

The answer seems obvious, yet a war is still raging on inside of me. It is difficult to give up on the life you've known, the life that you've grown to accept and enjoy. It is difficult to turn your back on a chance of a lifetime. And yet, that is exactly what I am considering right now.

She suddenly sighs, as if she, too has some inner struggle that she's trying to solve. "I probably shouldn't be telling you this," she says, and my curiosity immediately peaks, "but, she still has feelings for you. I mean, I'm shocked that you haven't figured this out on your own already."

"I was hoping that was the case," I admit.

"Well, hope will only get you so far, buddy," she snorts. "She might have been sending you mixed signals, but you know Elsie. You don't even need to assume stuff about her or guess. You were together, so you know how she functions."

"I do," I nod.

"So, stop being stupid then," she urges. "And do the right thing for once, whatever that right thing is in this case. If you guys won't be together, then have the balls to apologize properly and give her the closure she needs. If you guys will end up together, then again, admit you were wrong, apologize and go sweep her off her feet for fuck's sake!"

I almost chuckle out loud to her words. I notice that she's smiling, too.

"I know that this game is a big chance for you," she adds, and the strange thing is that she's been more of a friend to me in these several times that we've met than my other real friends have been in the past two years. "But remember that life is full of big chances. One goes, but the next one is just around the corner. And the one after that is as well. Don't be afraid to risk losing it all to gain it all."

She makes it sound so easy, so simple. I swallow heavily. "What if she won't have me?"

Rachel presses her lips together, shrugging. "That's the risk you're taking. There are no guarantees in life. I mean, who can guarantee that this big game will bring you exactly what you're hoping? It's a chance. Everything in life is a chance. You play it. You risk it. Sometimes you get exactly what you want. Other times, not. But you deal with it. You move on. That's what life is all about."

I grin. "You are way too young to be that wise."

"Life isn't measured by years," she shrugs. "But by bad experiences, and trust me, I've had a shitload of those. If I can give someone advice based on that and help them, it means that those shitty experiences weren't all in vain."

"That's a great way of looking at things," I tell her.

"It's easy to be the asshole in life," she reminds me. "We've all had shitty experiences. But that doesn't give us an excuse to treat others like we've been treated. A simple apology can get you a long way."

I nod to that. She's absolutely right. An apology would have probably saved us this entire mess. Then again, maybe if I left Elsie in a way that would have allowed her to move on, we wouldn't have gotten together again. I can't imagine that not happening. I feel like we were destined to meet again, even if it was just because of my shitty behavior.

"Well, I'd best be going now," she tells me, passing me by. "You think about what you want from your life, and then act on it."

She leaves me with those words, and for a moment, this whole conversation feels like it happened only inside my head. I'm alone behind the building, with no one else around. I feel dazed, confused, lost and the only light outside of this dark tunnel is her.

Elsie.

I want to go to her, but there's this constant fear that if she pushes me away, I will lose both things. Choosing the game means I might obtain my dream, then slowly, I could also try and get closer to her. Maybe that would be the best choice in this situation, the only certain choice.

I don't like to risk things. I never liked taking risks. I've always played it safe. I always prepared for everything I wanted, never expecting anything to just fall down from the skies, right into my lap. I was ready and still am to work for my professional success, just like I was ready and still am to work for Elsie's forgiveness. But she is the factor I can't control, while the end result of the game depends on me and how well I play. That is what I can control.

Still lost in thought, I head to the apartment, wondering what the right decision in this case is. Everything in me is telling me to go to Elsie. But what if she doesn't want me there at all? What if I will only make an already bad situation worse?

That night, I couldn't fall asleep, not that I was expecting to. I kept tossing and turning, my mind constantly replaying the good times Elsie and I had in the past, then reminding me of the horrible decision I made when I turned my back on her.

What for?

That question suddenly appears before me, and I realize that nothing I have now was worth her love, her smile, her tenderness.

I close my eyes tight, hoping that sleep would come, if only for a few hours. Eventually, somewhere right before dawn, it does. But it is not restful sleep. It is the kind of sleep that brings even more worry, even more reminders that you're either about to make the most wonderful decision of your life or that you're about to screw everything up... again.

Chapter Twenty-One

E lsie
I spent the night at the hospital, with mom. No amount of persuasion was enough to force me to go back to the dorm. This is where I wanted to be, and finally, she accepted it.

They've taken dad to be prepped for surgery about half an hour ago and advised us to go and eat something in the meantime, or maybe even rest. I almost laughed out loud when they told us this, as if such a thing was possible. My dad is having a surgery that might mean the difference between life and death, and they are suggesting I eat something. It's absolutely ridiculous.

Mom has been pacing about the waiting room for the past ten minutes. Then, she walks over to me and sits down.

I've been doing some people watching while we've been here. The waiting room of a hospital is never empty, it's never devoid of life. Sad life. Worried life. A life that has become ours now as well.

I recognize myself in every pair of eyes that I meet. We all share the same worry, the same concern for our loved ones, for ourselves. We all wonder what the future will look like. We are all afraid of what it might look like. Sometimes, it's easier just not to think about it, but it's not something you can easily forget. In fact, it's not something you can forget at all.

Mom sits down next to me. Neither of us speaks. We've run out of irrelevant things to talk about and discussing dad's operation is too difficult. The safest thing is just not to talk, to hide away in our own thoughts and hope for the best.

At that moment, I see Rachel walking into the waiting room, looking nervously about her. I immediately smile, raising my hand. She notices me, rushing over. I stand up, falling into her arms.

"You didn't need to come," I tell her when I finally pull away from her.

My mom smiles at her as well, and they hug, but both Rachel and I can tell that my mom's enthusiasm about hugging is not nearly as great as usual. This all has gotten to her, although she, just like dad, is putting on a brave face for both my sake as well as their own.

"You didn't think I'd miss this, did you?" Rachel asks, frowning a little at me. "Has the operation started?"

I look up at the clock, propped up onto the wall opposite us. It's five minutes past six o'clock. They should have started... hopefully. Rachel turns around and looks in the same direction. I don't need to tell her anything.

"You forgot to water your plants again," she tells me, pretending to be upset. "So, I had to do it again for you."

"Thanks," I manage a chuckle. It feels good to think about something else. "I don't even know why I keep them."

"Because you like them?" Rachel offers a reply. "Besides, they look nice on the windowsill. And I also have flowers, without actually admitting to having flowers."

"Aha," I nod, smiling. "Everything good at the dorm?"

I don't know why I'm even asking these stupid questions. I couldn't care less about what's going on at the dorm, but I feel like the silence is too oppressive. I need to talk about anything, other than the operation.

"Yeah," she nods. "Some pipes burst on the first floor last night, flooded the whole basement."

"Yikes," I say, grimacing.

"Yikes it is," she nods.

This is where neither of us knows how to continue this conversation, so we both sit down next to mom, staring into the distance. I keep thinking about dad. I wonder if he's frightened. I wonder how he's dealing with all the doubts and suspicions, all the fears and concerns.

I glance up at the clock again, and I realize that something else is taking place right now. Callum's big game. The one he's been waiting for. The one that could bring him closer to his ultimate goal.

I couldn't care less about the game, even if things were alright. But I do care about him. I realize how irrelevant all that is, when facing something so different, so life-altering. He broke my heart, but it's nothing that can't be mended. At least, that's what I believe now, in the face of this event that has me so tangled up. I face the horrific possibility of losing my father to cancer. Whether or not Callum was careless enough to break my heart again seems so insignificant, trivial even.

My mom suddenly gets up and starts pacing about the waiting room again. I realize that this soothes her. Motion. She can't handle sitting in one place and she needs motion to keep herself and her emotions under control.

At that moment, Rachel turns to me. The look on her face assures me that somehow, through some best friend magic, she is able to read my mind.

"I have to tell you something," she whispers, leaning closer to me. I scoot towards her on the bench.

"What is it?" I whisper back.

Rachel falters before continuing. "I spoke with Callum."

I frown. "Did he come looking for me again?"

I can't lie to myself. I can try to hide the truth from her, but I can't lie to myself, no matter how hard I try to. A part of me wants to hear a confirmation of this. I want to know that he's still trying to get to me, although everything I've been doing so far was to keep him away from me. Especially when I found out that he knew about my dad's condition.

That one hit me hard. I was already processing it in a very difficult way and realizing that he knew before me felt wrong in so many ways. I immediately resented him for not telling me. But if I had to think about it more deeply, I would probably do the same thing. I wouldn't tell the other person because it's not for me to reveal that.

I don't understand why everything about him has to be so complicated. There is nothing straightforward about him or any part of our relationship, whatever it may have been or is now. There is constant doubt, constant questioning, and I can't live like that. I don't want to.

That is why I think that, no matter how painful it might be now, the best decision for me, in the long run, is to stay away from him. I've managed to push him away, and he hasn't been trying to get in touch with me after we met at the hospital. I should just keep going down this path and focus on something else, anything else.

Dad will need me during his recovery process. The other possibility doesn't exist in my world. I refuse to accept it as such, which is why I know that I will concentrate on other things, more important things, and Callum Holland will forever fade from my mind and hopefully, my heart. Right now, that seems impossible, but I guess, in time, everything can become possible.

"He wasn't looking for you." Rachel's voice reaches me somewhere in the haze of my own thoughts and it pulls me back to the surface, forcing me to face reality once more. The disappointment of her statement stabs me.

He wasn't looking for you.

He has already given up, after just a few days. I know I shouldn't feel disappointed, but I do. I should be grateful, happy that I will be allowed to continue my life without him, once again. But I don't feel either joy or gratitude. There is just... emptiness. A big void, and a part of me wonders if I will ever trust a man again.

"I stumbled onto him while I was going back from class," she explains. "He asked about you, and I told him what's going on."

"I'm sure he knows way better than you," I say, frowning.

"He seemed really... lost somehow," she tells me, choosing to ignore my comment.

"Are you on his side?" I ask, gasping silently.

"No," she assures me. "Of course not. I'm always on your side, Elsie, always. I'm just telling you that this time, I saw a different side to Callum Holland, a side I never even thought he might have."

"Those might be just leftovers from the good guy that he used to be," I shrug. "But don't worry, he'll soon evaporate, leaving just this smug jock that we all know and don't really love."

Who am I kidding? I love him now as much as I loved him before, and it's all my fault that I allowed him, even invited him back into my life. He didn't ask for it. I agreed to it. I opened the door for him. All he had to do was walk through it, which he did. And now, I can't get him out of my system, no matter how many reasonable arguments I presented to myself about him.

"Well, you know him better than I do," she says.

"Did you tell him about dad's operation?" I ask.

"He asked," she answers apologetically.

I sigh. I can't even be mad at her. There's no point. Not like I could hide any of this, even if I tried my best. Everything is going downhill. I feel like I lost control of my entire life, and instead of improving my situation, things just keep piling up, threatening to suffocate me.

"It's fine," I assure Rachel, taking her by the hand. "Not like he'll appear here now. The game is too important."

Rachel doesn't say anything to that. I look down at my feet, resting against my knees. The silent chatter around us has gotten slightly louder, but I barely pay attention to it. There is enough loud chatter inside my mind, forcing me to keep my attention focused on it.

I hear the sound of oncoming footsteps, but I don't raise my gaze. The seconds are passing so slowly. They feel as long as hours.

The footsteps are coming closer. My heart flutters, thinking it's the doctor, coming with news, although I know it's still too early. They couldn't have good news, not only fifteen minutes or so into the surgery. That might mean that they had bad news, and bad news would mean–

"Elsie?"

I swallow heavily, raising my gaze to meet Callum's. He is the last person I need here. But at the same time, he is the one I need here.

I feel like my throat is dry. It's parched. I look around, mom is still wandering. She's walked over to the window, gazing at something outside, something to distract her.

Rachel gets up. I expect her to push him away, to shout at him, as much as she can shout at a hospital, but she surprises me when she does none of those things. Instead, she tells me something even more incredulous.

"I'll go get us all some coffee," she says, insinuating that she wants to give us some privacy.

Once again, privacy is the last thing I need with this guy. And yet, I can't tell him to go away, when every fiber of my being wants to wrap my arms around him and just get lost in his embrace, inhaling his scent.

I wait for Rachel to walk over to my mom. She whispers something to her. My mom shakes her head. She throws a casual glance in my direction. But I feel like she's not even seeing me, like she's looking through me, not at me. I know that feeling of helplessness, because I have succumbed to it as well.

Rachel passes us by one more time as she heads down the hallway and out of sight. Then, I finally turn to him, trying to sound as grave as possible, while my heart is threatening to betray me.

"What do you want?"

Chapter Twenty-Two

Callum

I feel like my entire body is trembling, as I'm standing before her, almost as if I'm naked. In a way, I've come to bare not only my emotions, but also my entire self to her. That is the only way to show her my true emotions, those same emotions that I've been sweeping under the metaphorical carpet for so long. But with her reappearance in my life, I can't deny any of that any longer.

She looks at me, disbelievingly. I feel like an apparition that has to prove its presence to a human, but itself isn't completely sure that it exists.

"If you came to talk to me about that stupid kiss again, I swear– "

"No," I interrupt her, taking a seat next to her. Her presence both comforts me, and it thrills me at the same time. It's hard to resist the temptation to hug her, to touch her, to kiss her. "I didn't come to talk about that stupid kiss, because that is exactly what it is. A stupid kiss. And as such, it doesn't matter."

"Fine," she says.

I can hear the defiance in her voice. That's how she always was when she felt vulnerable, when she didn't want others to know how powerless she felt.

"I came... just to be here, with you," I say, realizing how stupid and completely lacking in common sense that sounds. But it's the truth. That's the only reason I'm here. So, I continue. "I didn't come to apologize, although if you want me to, I will do it over and over again. I know I messed up. But I don't want to bother you with unimportant things right now. All that matters now is for your dad to get better. You shouldn't think about anything else other than that."

I expect her to snarl something back at me, but she doesn't. She listened, and the words somehow reached her. I don't know how, but I'm not questioning it.

"Why did you keep it a secret from me?" she asks.

I've dreaded this question, but in order for her to fully forgive me for everything, I need to explain this as well. I can't have any more secrets before her.

"Your dad asked me not to tell you," I reveal. "But, even if he didn't, I probably wouldn't tell you, so don't blame him."

"I would never blame my dad," she says, looking down at her feet. She has her fingers crossed between her knees, focusing on something other than our conversation. "But I blame you for not telling me."

"Blame me," I nod. "Blame me for everything, I deserve it. I won't deny that. I've made more mistakes than I can count or account for. But I'm here. I don't know if that counts for anything. I'm not here to be forgiven. I'm here just to be here, with you," I repeat.

She lifts her gaze. It locks with mine.

"What about the game?" she suddenly asks.

That question feels like a punch in the gut. "What about the game?"

"It's on, isn't it?"

I nod. If I close my eyes, I can hear the chanting, all the sounds. I can see all my teammates, running around the field under the big lights, all waiting for that one chance. I can see it all. And yet, I can't see myself there, as if that isn't where I belong.

"Shouldn't you be there instead?"

"Do you think that is where I belong?" I wonder. I want her to tell me this.

"Does it matter what I think?" She answers my question with another question, refusing to answer. But I know that refusal stems from fear. Fear of opening up again, fear of getting hurt. And it's all my fault. I pushed her into this state, first by dumping her in a way that no one deserves to be dumped, and then by telling her one thing but showing her another, by being caught kissing another girl, although she kissed me. But that is just an excuse. It was a kiss that never should have happened. I need to accept responsibility for it and recognize it as my own mistake, and not the mistake that was forced onto me.

"Of course, it matters," I tell her. "I feel like that is the only thing that ever mattered, but I was stupid enough not to see it."

For a moment it seems like she might smile, but she doesn't. Her face seems stern, as if she is determined to hide all the emotions deep down inside of her, not allowing them to come to the surface, at least not in front of me.

"Isn't it your dream to play in the big leagues?" she reminds me. "This is your big chance. You could still probably make it."

"I don't want to make it," I finally tell her exactly what I mean, exactly what I want and don't want. "I want to stay here, with you."

"What if I don't want you here?" she dares me.

Her cheeks flush slightly. This always happened when she was arguing with someone. Even in such situations, she never wanted to hurt anyone, and felt bad that she was attacking someone, even if it was just with words. Her kind soul could never agree with that.

"In that case..." I start, wondering what the right course of action in those circumstances would be. "I would still stay, not for you, but for your dad and mom. I don't know them that well, but I know they are good people. I want to hear the outcome of the operation. And when I hear that, I will leave. You will never see me again, if that is what you want."

She bites her lower lip, as if in an effort to prevent herself from saying something she might regret.

"If there is anything you wish to tell me, anything..." I urge. "Now is the time, Elsie."

"I know what I want," she admits softly, muttering under her breath, refusing to look me in the eye. "I'm just afraid that it might lead to more heartache."

"You need promises?" I ask. "Guarantees?"

She shrugs.

"Life is unpredictable, Elsie. You know this yourself," I start. "You can't control it. But you can control how you react to what life throws at you. So, if promises are what you need, promises are what I can give you. Promises that I will never hurt you again. Promises that I will never take you for granted again. Promises that I will cherish you."

"What about guarantees?" She reminds me of the other word I used, and there is a faint glimmer of a snicker on her face.

"Well," I smile, "I can guarantee all that, as well."

This time, she chuckles, and it feels like the sun itself managed to squeeze into the waiting room through those narrow windows and shine right upon me. I can't believe how I managed to live without her smile and voice all this time. But now I know that I don't want to live a single moment more without her.

Dreams or no dreams. Goals or no goals.

Sometimes, sacrifices have to be made for the greater good. And Elsie is that greater good for me. She is the one I want. She is the one I always wanted but was too stupid to realize and I lost her once. But I don't plan on making that mistake again.

This time, I dare to reach for her and take her hand. I half-expect her to pull away, but she doesn't. She allows me to hold her.

"I've been an idiot," I say it in the simplest words I can think of. It works. My admission makes her smile. "I know it's too much to ask, but if you forgive me, I'll spend the rest of my life making it up to you."

She gazes at me. I look deeply into her eyes, trying to find the answer to my question, but her eyes are fathomless. I look down at her lips, they aren't moving. She is expressionless. Perhaps I have crossed the line. I shouldn't have pushed for it so quickly. All these thoughts start swarming inside my mind, quick and angry, like arrows. And before I can make any sense of them, she presses her lips to mine.

There is nothing sexual about that kiss. It is a kiss of promise, of belonging, of forgiveness. A kiss that signals that once again, our two hearts are beating as one. I close my eyes, enjoying the moment, when I hear someone's voice interrupt us.

"Oh, come on guys. This is a hospital."

Elsie pulls away from me, and I immediately see Rachel standing in front of us, her hands on her hips, like a nanny about to scold a naughty child for something he's done.

"So, I see you've worked it out," she continues, sitting on Elsie's other side. She is carrying three cups of coffee and offers us both one. I accept first, then Elsie. "Or you're well on your way there."

I notice Elsie blushes. I want to reach over and caress her cheek, to feel that warmth, but I resist the temptation.

At that moment, Elsie's mom approaches, and we exchange a cordial greeting and a few pleasantries. I explain that I've come here to support Elsie, and her mom feels overwhelmed by this. The conversation somehow gets steered to less serious topics, and we all take part in it.

All the while, I can't take my eyes off Elsie. She occasionally steals a few glances, too. I know there are still so many things that are left unsaid, but I'm glad that she has opened herself up to me once again. This time, I know I can't let her down.

As for my own promise to myself and my goals, those would need to wait. There will always be chances to play pro football, if I can prove myself worthy of that chance, which I believe I am. But this time, there was something far more worthy I needed to prove myself for. And I managed to do it.

I remember my time at the hospital during my grandad's stay, and I fear that I will get overwhelmed by negative feelings. Instead, every time I look in Elsie's direction, her very presence comforts me. It reminds me that sometimes we forget what our real priorities in life are. I know I might be back at the game now. I might be listening to the whole stadium cheering my name. I might be on my way to the big leagues. I might be doing all that right now. But I'm not, nor do I have any such plans.

Right now, I am exactly where I need to be. I feel it deep down inside of me, in my very bones. Once, I almost lost what truly matters in life. Now, through some fluke of good luck, I had another chance at happiness, and I had no intention of letting it slip away from me again.

"Mrs. Medina?"

Suddenly, our conversation is interrupted by a serious-sounding voice that belongs to a doctor, who was still wearing his green garb and a mask over his face.

The moment we all looked in his direction, he pulls the mask from around his right ear first, then his left ear, revealing his face and a thin moustache he seemed to be growing out. There is nothing in his facial expression that is helping us determine whether the operation was a success or not.

I remember everything. I know how Elsie feels. Without thinking, I take her by the hand, squeezing it gently. I want her to know that I'm here, that I won't be going anywhere. She squeezes it back but doesn't look at me. Her eyes are focused on the doctor and what his next words are going to be.

"The operation is finished."

Chapter Twenty-Three

Elsie

I listen as the doctor explains in layman's words what they did, but that's not what I want to hear. Eagerly, I drink in his words, as Callum holds me by the hand and it feels like the most natural thing in the world, as if our hands were always meant to be together like that.

Then, finally, the doctor tells us what we've been dying to hear.

"We believe we managed to get all the cancerous tissue out," he says. "There is still the recovery process, but it is safe to say that Mr. Medina will be alright."

My mom presses her hand to her lips, to suppress a gasp of relief, but she can't hide her smile. Neither can I.

"Oh, thank goodness," she whispers, more to herself than to any of us. "When can we see him?"

"He is still under the effects of anesthesia, but he should be out of it soon," he tells her. "I can have the nurse come for you when he regains consciousness."

"Yes, thank you," my mom nods quickly. "Thank you so much."

The doctor smiles, then retreats without another word, and mom turns to us. I feel like we've all aged at least five years throughout this ordeal, but it's mostly noticeable on her and her usually youthful visage. It was up to her to bear the brunt of it all.

"I can't wait to hug your father," she tells me, with a trembling voice. Then, she turns to Rachel and Callum. "And you two are so sweet to come and be Elsie's moral support. It warms my heart to know that she has such people to care for her, when we're not around."

This is definitely not the moment to explain to my mother that Callum and I have only gotten back together, after much turmoil, so I just smile back.

"Maybe now we could all go to the cafeteria for some food?" I suggest, not really because I'm hungry, but because waiting here for another half an hour or more until dad wakes up will drive me crazy. Just a slight change of scenery, still inside the hospital, might prevent that.

"I could eat," Rachel says first.

"I probably won't," mom replies. "But I can keep you company."

Callum nods, and all four of us head to the cafeteria. I order a small sandwich, and the moment I take the first bite, hunger returns with a vengeance. I don't even notice it, but I wolf down both the sandwich and the coffee I had with it. It seems that everyone's appetite opened up a bit. After that, we exchange a few superficial pleasantries, returning to the waiting room.

About fifteen minutes later, the nurse arrives, informing us that dad is still weak and drowsy, but mom and I can go in to see him, for just a few minutes.

"You just go on ahead," Rachel urges. "Callum and I will wait out here."

I smile at her, taking my mom by the hand. Together, we walk back to dad's room, knocking on the door softly, and only then opening the door. The room is bathed in the soft glow of the late afternoon sun, whose rays are oozing through the window to the right of the bed. Dad is lying, covered up to his chest. There is an IV still attached to his arm. His head is propped up with the pillow. His eyes are open, and he notices us immediately upon our arrival.

"Hey girls," he says a bit drowsily as we walk over to the bed, standing on either side of it and taking him by the hand. It feels so cold, so clammy.

"How was it?" mom asks.

He shrugs. "I barely felt it," he replies, making us chuckle.

"Are you in any pain now?" I ask.

"No," he assures me, but I don't know if he's only telling me that because it's what I wish to hear. "The painkillers have already kicked in."

"That's good," I smile.

"The doctor told us the surgery was a success," mom says.

"See?" he comments. "That only proves my point that you girls were blowing this way out of proportion. We shouldn't have told you, Elsie. We worried you over nothing."

"That's not true, dad," I reply. "Besides, it seems that there's another person who knew, but who shouldn't have known."

Maybe I shouldn't have mentioned this, but the need is stronger than the desire to keep quiet about it.

"Oh." That's all he says, but in a way that almost makes me burst out into laughter. Not that it matters anymore anyway, but still.

"I found out from Callum that he stumbled onto you at the hospital," I explain. From the look on mom's face, it seems like she also didn't know.

"Yes, I did," dad nods, admitting. "It was during the first tests. You know I always liked the guy, even though I only met him a few times. But I don't like him that much to spill the beans first to him and then to you."

"Well, that's what happened," I say. "I'm not upset, just..."

"I know," he tells me. "I didn't handle this well at all. But I stumbled onto him by accident. Literally bumped into him. All my test results fell to the floor. I could see that he was trying his best not to look at them, but he bent down to help me pick them up and... I mean, he's not blind. He's got eyes. You can not want to see, but that doesn't mean you won't see." He sighs a little, then continues. "So, I asked him not to tell you anything. I know you aren't dating anymore, so you probably don't see each other, but I didn't want you to find out from him."

"I understand," I nod. "Thank you for explaining."

"I just wanted to keep you out of all this, for your own sake," he adds.

"I know," I smile. "It was done with the best intentions in mind."

"Exactly," he confirms.

"Also, you're wrong about one thing, darling," mom suddenly interferes, with a sly look in her eyes.

"What do you mean?" he wonders, lifting his eyebrow at her.

"About the dating part," she clarifies. "They weren't dating, but I think they are now."

Dad turns to me, with the same sort of smile. "Is that true?"

My lips part, but I feel like this isn't the right time for this conversation. So, I exhale loudly first, then I reply. "It's true, but... it's complicated."

"What's complicated about it?" mom voices her question. "You either want to be with him or not. You will either do everything in your power to have him by your side or you won't. Love is never complicated, darling. It's actually very simple."

And just like that, I realize she's right. We're always trying to make it seem like love is this complicated sensation, and it is making us even more confused when we accept the fact that we love someone. But the truth is that you either love someone or you don't. There is no in between. There is no questioning about it. You can't imagine your life without that person, and that is how you know that nothing else and no one else could ever do.

I know why I've been so reluctant to accept the fact that I still love him. He hurt me beyond words. He left me, not because I did something, but simply because of who I was, and it seemed that I wasn't who he wanted. Knowing that, broke me. It completely and utterly destroyed me, and it took me a long time to start functioning properly again, going out again among people and behaving like my old self.

Sleeping with him was supposed to be a test that I wanted to put my own self on. I wanted to prove to myself that I was over him, that

I could sleep with him without stirring all those passions up again. But I was wrong. I wasn't over him. The only thing I managed to do was just sweep all my emotions underneath the carpet and keep them there, pretending that I was free of them. But seeing him, touching him, kissing him, stirred up the old flames and now, the fire burns brighter than ever.

A part of me is still afraid. But I know that all things worth living for come with a certain amount of risk. And I'm ready to take it on.

"Do you know that your grandma, God rest her soul, hated your father at first?" mom suddenly asked me.

My eyes widen in shock. "That can't be," I shake my head. "Grandma loved dad."

I remember all the times she called dad when she needed something to be fixed around the house, and she would always welcome him like her own son. There was not a single instance of animosity in her behavior towards him.

"Later, yes," mom nodded. "But initially, she thought he wasn't good enough for me."

"Heck, I still think that," dad suddenly interrupts, making mom chuckle. "You are too good for me, darling. You always have been, and your mom knew it, but she pretended to like me, for your sake."

"I'm trying to make a point here," mom scolded him playfully. "Grandma accepted dad, and when she saw the kind of man he was, the kind of man I fell in love with, she could do nothing else but love him as well. Still, that didn't mean that she didn't try to keep us apart in the beginning."

"Really?" I ask, all incredulous. "I can't believe grandma did that."

"Oh, you better believe it," dad nodded. "It's all true. She always came up with all sorts of excuses not to let your mom come meet me, always finding obligations. Several times she even downright forbade her from seeing me."

"What did you do?" I ask mom.

"Isn't that obvious?" mom asks, leaning over dad and planting a soft kiss on his forehead. "I did exactly what I felt I needed to do. And I know it was the right thing, although your grandma tried to convince me I was wrong. But I fought for the one I wanted, the one I loved. And I can't imagine ever loving anyone else. If that is how you feel about Callum, then you shouldn't be confused at all. You shouldn't allow anything or anyone to stand in your way and to convince you of something you know is right for you."

I remember the kiss. Callum told me he didn't kiss her back. She kissed him. Maybe it wasn't just an excuse.

I sigh heavily, and dad immediately catches the hint.

"Now is probably not the time to talk about that," he advises. "Elsie must be overwhelmed by what happened here, with me. Making huge, life-altering decisions right this moment might not be advisable."

"Thanks, dad," I smile. "But I actually think mom is right."

"I am?" mom wonders, then makes one of her funny, confident faces. "Of course, I am."

I giggle. "I'm just afraid, that's all. But I shouldn't live my life in fear."

"That is the worst way to live your life, darling," dad reminds me.

"I know," I agree. "I should learn to take more risks, and to believe in myself."

"Even if you make a mistake, it's OK," mom adds. "We all make mistakes, and that is how we learn. Sometimes, the path we choose isn't the right path after all, and there is nothing wrong starting all over from scratch. It's much better than continuing to go along a path you will eventually despise. But by the time you've had enough, it will be too late to change anything."

"Speaking of change..." I realize that if we're talking about life-altering decisions, I might as well say what's been lying heavily on my heart. "There's something I've been wanting to tell you, but I've been afraid to."

"Afraid?" mom asks, sounding doubtful. "Why would you ever be afraid to talk to us about anything?"

"Because I'm afraid I might disappoint you..."

"You could never disappoint us, darling," mom tells me lovingly. "Never."

"I..." I inhale deeply, mustering the courage. "I think I might want to change my major, or maybe even enroll to a different college."

Mom frowns. She glances at dad, then back at me. "That's all?" she asks, anticlimactically.

"Well... yes," I nod, not sure if I should smile or frown.

Mom suddenly bursts into laughter. "You silly thing," she tells me. "That should be the smallest of your concerns. If you think you want to do something else with your life, then you go and do it. Dad and I support you all the way, whatever choice you make."

We huddle together in a family hug, and I feel that overwhelming sensation of wanting to cry, but there are no tears. My heart is filled with joy, and I know that finally, everything will be alright.

Chapter Twenty-Four

Callum

I drive Rachel and Elsie back to their dorm. The ride back is silent. All three of us seem lost in our thoughts, with the radio filling the silent void pleasantly with enough sound to distract us. When we reach our destination, Rachel gets out first. She waits for Elsie, but Elsie hesitates in the car. I recognize that sign immediately. She wants to say something but doesn't really know how.

Hope flares up inside of me. I don't want to let go of her. Not now that everything is alright again, or at least, very close to being alright again. I want to assure her that there is nothing to be afraid of, that I realized my mistake, and that I will do everything in my power to keep her safe and loved. All these thoughts are swarming inside my mind, but I can't say a single thing of it out loud.

"Do you uhm... maybe want to hang out tonight?" I ask. An alarm inside my mind gets turned on immediately. "I'm not asking because of sex, just... maybe... if you want to talk or..."

"Sure," she smiles, interrupting my completely nonsensical train of thought, with which I'm not even sure what I was trying to say. I don't want her to think that I'm inviting her over just for sex, because it's far from it. Yet, I still somehow feel that we didn't get to discuss everything properly, and the hospital was the last place where such conversations should be held.

Elsie leans out of the car to speak to Rachel, but she's already chuckling to herself. Obviously, she knows what's going on.

"I heard it," Rachel says, rolling her eyes, as if she were annoyed, but the look on her face reveals otherwise. "Have fun, love birds."

She blows a kiss to Elsie, then heads inside the dorm. Elsie slams the door shut, placing her hands in her lap.

"We could order a pizza and watch a movie?" she suggests.

"Sounds great," I nod, stepping on the gas and taking us back to my place.

About an hour later, we're seated comfortably at my kitchen table. There is an open pizza box. Half of it is already missing. Two cans of Coke stand on each side. Elsie is seated opposite me, with one foot on the chair, her knee at the level of her chin, and she would occasionally rest her head on it, as she watches me.

We haven't really spoken much since arriving here. The pizza got here quickly, and I felt starved at the very smell of fast food.

"What do you think your coach will say?" she suddenly asks.

I swallow the last bite I was chewing on, before replying.

"I have no idea," I tell her. "I had a few missed calls from him. I didn't pick up."

"That probably won't make things better," she notices.

"I don't doubt that," I confirm.

"I feel guilty about this," she says softly. "I mean, it's because of me that you not only missed a golden opportunity, but you'll be in trouble now as well."

"None of this is your fault," I assure her. "If anything, it's mine. Completely mine. No one else's. I know that now, and I don't want to have anyone else take responsibility for my mistakes."

She doesn't seem convinced. So, I get up and walk over to her. I take her by the hand and help her stand up, so that she's now facing me. She looks straight at me, those big blue eyes constantly trying to understand something.

"None of that matters," I tell her, cupping her chin with my fingers. "That is a goal I can obtain later, but if I lost you now, I knew that I would lose you forever. I made the mistake of letting you go once. I couldn't be so stupid to make the same mistake again, no matter what the price was."

"What if another chance to play in the pro league doesn't present itself?" she asks.

I know what she is afraid of. She is fearful that her love will cost me my dream, and it happens often that people who have given up their dream become bitter and upset with others, especially those who cost them that dream. But I can't imagine this ever happening. Not with us.

"It will," I tell her, smiling. "And I'll just tell coach I had a medical emergency in the family. It will be fine. Now that I have you, I know everything will be fine."

With those words, I press my lips to hers. She trembles softly. My body longs for her, but I don't want her to think that is the only thing I'm interested in. Even now, that everything is said and done, I want her to know that I value her, that I cherish her, that I...

"I love you," I pull away suddenly, saying those words for the first time.

She seems taken aback. She obviously wasn't expecting me to say it. But I'm not sorry. I don't regret it. When we were dating before, we didn't say those words. I could see them, though, in everything she did, but she didn't want to be the first one to say them. And I was OK with that, because I wasn't sure how I felt. When I say those words to someone, I wanted it to mean something. I wanted it to be profound and meaningful. I wanted it to last forever.

Now that I said them out loud, I realize all of this is true. The words are profound and meaningful. And I want them to last forever.

Her lower lip trembles as she gazes at me, her eyes fathomless and deep. The full gravity of what I've done to her hits me all at once. I betrayed her. I betrayed her heart. And yet, she is here, with me, looking at me with those loving eyes. I realize that she is my heavenward guide. She always wanted what was the best for me. She always kept me on the right path, helping me focus on my true life's mission, and I chose not to be faithful to her.

I feel as if I've been ruled by an evil force all this time, almost as if I sold my own soul, and her heart paid the price.

"I love you," I repeat, "and I am so sorry for all the pain that I have caused you. I want to spend the rest of my life making it up to you." I know I already told her this once, but I want to keep repeating it until she is completely assured of the truth of those words.

She is still looking at me, silent. She is radiant with love, that quiet emotion which she always possessed and so unselfishly shared with me, until I pushed her away. But in time, she became part of the oxygen I need to breathe. When she was no longer around, I felt that removal, I felt like an invisible hand was choking me at times and I wasn't able to breathe. That was when I would bury myself in booze, in girls, in drunken nights I couldn't remember, just because something vital was missing from my life, and I couldn't figure out what that was. But here I am now, gazing into her eyes, and everything becomes crystal clear.

"I love you, too," she whispers to me, her hand resting on my cheek, caressing it. "I never stopped loving you."

Unable to hold myself back, I take her into my arms, our lips pressed against each other, our hearts beating as one. My mind is telling me to pull away, to take it easy, to take it slowly, but my heart is unable to stop beating for her.

As if sensing my desire, my love, she grabs me by the shirt collar, pulling me even closer to her. We stumble backward, towards the table, and she sits up on it, spreading her legs around my waist. My dick is threatening to tear my zipper to shreds.

"I love you..." I keep telling her through soft breaths we need to take between kisses. Her heavy breathing is enough of a response, as she is clutching onto me desperately, as if afraid that I might disappear again. My fingers dig into her flesh, as if marred by the same fear.

"I love you," I say again and again, as she unzips my pants. They drop down to the ground. She fumbles with my boxer shorts, pulling them down just a little.

"I love you, too," she says, her lips pressed to mine. I can feel her warm breath on my cheek, as she takes off her own pants and underwear, then again locks her legs around me, pulling me closer to herself.

I can feel the warmth of her desire, oozing. My tip presses against her wet pussy. Our cheeks are pressed together. She moans softly into my ear, and it drives me crazy. I'm almost afraid to slide into her. I know I won't be able to handle much. I'm more turned on than ever before. A part of me wants to prolong this moment, but another part of me wants to get lost in the blissful state of ecstasy with her.

"Fuck me," she whispers, and that single statement pushes me over the edge.

I slide into her, as her fingers dig into my ass, pulling me closer. Her breathing has become ragged, frantic. I fuck her on the table, as she arches her back, exposing the soft lines of her throat. Her hands fly back behind her, propping herself up, while her legs are still locked around me.

"I love you," I say again, realizing that even if I said it a million times in the next few minutes, it still wouldn't be enough. "You are mine..."

She moans loudly this time, biting her lower lip, her eyes closed. Her entire body is trembling, and so is mine. I can't prolong this sweet torture any longer.

I thrust heavily a few more times, sliding into her heat every time, regretting having to pull out, when I just want to go in deeper and deeper. Our breaths have become shallow. I swallow heavily, grabbing onto her as if grabbing for my dear life, because that is what she is. She is life. She is light. She is love.

Two more thrusts and I explode on her right thigh, spilling my hot seed onto her naked flesh. She looks down, her lips parted, her cheeks flushed. When our eyes meet, she smiles shyly, and I kiss her tenderly. There is no tongue, just lips, just the sweet sensation of her plumpness against my ragged breath.

I press my sweaty forehead against hers, gathering my breath. She is still not letting go of me. That's fine, because I don't want to let go of her either. If I could, I would stay like this forever.

"So, what movie you wanna watch?" she asks, and a moment later, we both burst out into laughter.

I pull away and she slides off. "Sorry about sitting on your table," she tells me.

"You're kidding, right?" I chuckle. "That's the best use I put that table to since the first day of me living here."

She smiles, then reaches for another slice of pizza. "I was thinking we could watch an old classic or something."

I smile back. "I think classics are the best."

"You can always go back to them, knowing what to expect. After all, they are classics for a reason, no?" she chuckles.

The sound of her laughter is something I never want to be without again. I clean myself off, then we finish the rest of the pizza, talking about unimportant things, and I know there is nowhere else I would rather be, than here with her. As for playing pro, that's still something to think about. But the future is more than just ambition. The future is being happy. And ambition alone rarely makes someone a happy man.

We spend that evening in my bed with a movie I barely paid any attention to. She is the only thing that occupied all my senses, and every once in a while, I still felt overwhelmed by the fact that I am that lucky guy who gets to sleep next to her every night.

Epilogue – Three Years Later

Elsie

I look down at my hand. The ring is beautiful. It is exactly what I would have chosen if Callum had asked me what I would have liked. But somehow, he managed to figure it out on his own. It is a dainty pear-shaped diamond, with a frame of tiny little crystals. Ever since Callum has given it to me, I can't stop looking at it, admiring it, reminding myself what it truly means.

He is sitting opposite me at the table. The restaurant isn't crowded, but we still had to make reservations ahead of time, mostly because this is my mom's favorite restaurant in the city. This is where dad took her on their first proper date, as he likes to call it. This is also where they took grandma and grandpa to tell them that they were having a baby. This is also where we had lunch after the first tests after the surgery showed a negative biopsy result. Now, Callum and I will continue the tradition. This will be the place where we will tell my parents that we are getting married.

The waiter stops by and brings us our drinks. He places an orange juice in front of me, and a coffee with sparkling water for Callum.

"Thanks," I smile at the waiter. He returns the smile, then disappears, as we already informed him that we are waiting for the rest of our party to arrive, and then we'll all order together.

I look across the table at Callum. He is wearing a light blue polo shirt, and with his slight tan, it looks perfect on him. I noticed a few women threw curious glances at him when we passed. I don't notice it often. Also, I don't mind. I trust him completely, and he trusts me. Without that trust, we wouldn't be able to get over the things that were standing between us and reach the place where we are now. The perfect place of love and understanding.

"I don't know why they're late," I say apologetically, looking around, expecting to see the familiar faces of my parents, but they are still nowhere to be seen.

"Relax," Callum tells me. "It's probably the traffic or something. They're on their way."

"You're right," I say, nodding.

Even though three years have passed since dad's operation, I still get these panic attacks where the worst kind of thoughts occupy every corner of my mind, and I can't get them out of my head. I start thinking that something must have happened to dad, and mom had to call the ambulance, and that's why they are late, or that's why they aren't picking up their phone exactly at the moment when I'm calling them.

But luckily, I have Callum to tell me that I'm exaggerating. He reminds me that I'm crossing the line of worry and delving into paranoid territory, which I don't want to do.

So, as always, I listen to him as his words bring me back to reality, focusing on the present moment, on the fact that everything is alright. And it is. There is nothing to fear.

He smiles at me from across the table, and it hits me once again how fortunate we both are that we didn't allow the past to dictate our present. He made a mistake. He made more than one mistake, to be honest. But perhaps, it was that mistake, which was necessary to separate us, so we could grow apart and also grow as individual human beings, independent of each other. As it turned out, we still found our way back to each other, and that just proves that sometimes, a couple is meant to be, even when all the pieces of the puzzle do not seem to be a match from the onset.

"You look gorgeous," he suddenly tells me, making me blush.

"Thanks," I smile looking down at my lap, glad that I chose this flowery dress for the special occasion.

"As soon as they see you, they'll know we invited them for lunch with a hidden agenda in mind," he teases.

"I doubt I'll be able to keep my mouth shut for longer than three seconds," I admit through a chuckle. "I'll be like, hey, how are you, I'm good and engaged!"

My words make him laugh, and at that moment exactly, I notice my mom coming through the main entrance, with dad following closely behind. She waves at me, and they both head in our direction.

"That darn traffic," dad comments as soon as they reach our table. "I always forget how busy it is in the city."

Both Callum and I get up, greeting my parents cordially. My mom wraps her arms around me, then releases me from her grip, but keeps her hands on my shoulders.

"Something is different about you," she says, and I almost gasp aloud at her words. "New haircut? No." She shakes her head. "It's not that." Then, her gaze travels down to my hand, and she immediately sees it. "You have a ring. An engagement ring. Oh, my gosh, John," she turns to dad, her eyes wide with shock and joy, "Elsie is engaged!!"

My dad's face shows an equal amount of disbelief, but all Callum and I can do is burst into laughter. Mom and dad immediately huddle around me, like a hen and a rooster safeguarding an egg. My mom is kissing my cheek, while my dad is hugging me. Then, they switch. It's all a spectacle, and I know the whole restaurant is watching, wondering who the heck these weirdos are, but I don't care.

Then, once I'm done, it's Callum's turn. I didn't think that they would give him the same treatment, but they do. My mom hugs him and showers him with kisses, while dad hugs him and shakes his hand. All this seems to last a small eternity, when we finally all sit down, and are able to talk again.

Mom's eyes are constantly jumping from me to Callum, then back at me again. A smile hasn't left her lips since she found out about the engagement.

"You know, I was hoping to be the one to surprise you with the news," I tell them, not feeling even the slightest bit disappointed with how things went down. The reaction is the same, and it is exactly the reaction I was hoping to get from them.

"You did surprise us," mom points out. "I just saw the ring before you could tell us about it."

"Your mother is like that, honey," dad interferes, teasing. "She sees both the things she's supposed to see and things she's not supposed to see. In fact, I think she sees more of the latter."

Mom shoots him a playfully scornful gaze, then chuckles out loud.

"Do you like it?" I ask them, showing them the ring.

Mom, who is seated to my left, takes my hand into hers, and makes a close inspection of the ring. "It's absolutely stunning," she comments.

"Isn't it?" I agree. "Callum chose it himself."

"Well done, Callum," dad congratulates him. "Guessing your lady's preferred jewelry is a skill not many men have."

"Do you have it?" I ask, smiling.

"Do you even need to ask that?" dad wonders, giving mom a meaningful glance. "I'll just let your mother answer that question."

"Yes," mom replies, rolling her eyes, although we can all see she's doing it to play along. "Your father likes to toot his own horn, but in this case, it's true. I love all the jewelry he has gotten me over the years, especially my engagement ring."

I glance back at dad. He is all smug and important, and that makes it all the more fun. The waiter arrives a moment later, offering us the menus. We spend some time perusing them, then we make our choice and order.

"Have you given any thought to the wedding yet?" mom asks, taking a sip of her lemonade.

"Well," I look at Callum, who's allowed me to handle all the questions and arrangements regarding the wedding. His words were that he wants the kind of wedding that I want. Fortunately, we met somewhere in the middle, with a small group of close people at a small venue. This is what I share with my parents, and they both seem to love the idea.

"You could have the wedding at our house," mom suggests, looking at both of us. "In the back yard. There's more than enough space."

"Oh, I'm not sure," I shrug, glancing at Callum.

We haven't discussed the possibility of it being at my parents' place, although the thought did occur to me.

"I don't want to occupy your home or make a mess of it," I explain.

"It's no problem," mom assures me. "We'd love to host it, if that is what you want."

I can see it in her eyes, the desire to have her only daughter's wedding in the house where she grew up, in the house where she made her first steps and where she snuck out of the window, which hopefully, those same parents know nothing about.

"Callum?" mom calls out to him, as she sees that I'm indecisive about it.

Callum seems to ponder it for a moment, then smiles. "I think that's a great idea, Mrs. Medina."

"Oh please," she waves her hand at him dismissively. "We're practically family already. Please, call me Stephie."

"Stephie," he does as he's told, "I think that is a great idea," he repeats.

"Then, it's settled!" Mom claps her hands joyfully. "I can't wait to let everyone know."

"We have to plan it first, mom," I remind her, laughing.

"Of course, of course," she nods at me.

The conversation stays on that topic for a while longer, then dad and Callum hit it off, as they usually do, talking about football and other guy stuff, leaving the wedding planning to the women.

That night, as we're lying in bed, cuddling, I lift my gaze, looking up at Callum. It seems that neither of us is yet ready for sleep, although it's dark in the room, with only one nightlight turned on.

"I'm sorry my mom put you on the spot like that today," I tell him.

"What do you mean?" he asks, raising his eyebrow.

"The wedding location," I remind him.

"Oh," he nods. "That. It's fine."

"You don't have to agree just because she offered, you know. We could have it anywhere else, wherever you want it to be."

"Why do you think I wouldn't want to have it there?" He seems confused.

"I don't know," I shrug, and since I'm lying down, it's a weird movement. "I thought maybe you agreed just because everyone expected you to."

"I wouldn't bow down to pressure, if that's what you're referring to," he explains. "I agreed because I really think it would be a lovely place to have the wedding. It's your home. It's where you grew up. It's where you feel the best. And if you feel the best there, then I feel the same way."

His words bring me so much joy. I stretch a little to get my lips closer to his, then I kiss him.

"Can you imagine?" I whisper. "We'll be husband and wife."

"I know of a husband and wife game we could play right now," he whispers back into my neck, tickling me as he does, which makes me giggle. His whispers turn into soft kisses, and I know exactly where he's going with this.

"Tell me more about this game," I moan softly, moving myself closer to him, as he wraps up his arms around me.

Once we are done, he falls asleep immediately. His arm is bent around my waist, as we spoon together. I listen to the deep, comforting sounds of his breathing, but I can't fall asleep. Some nights are just like this. I am kept up by the sheer desire to stay up, to ponder on my own happiness as well as the happiness that is yet to come, with the man my heart has chosen to be my life companion.

I always remember how there was once the possibility of losing him, and it only makes me value and cherish him more. The love I feel for him is undying. And I know he feels the same way about me. The past wasn't able to break us or keep us apart. If anything, it brought us back together. And this time, our love was enough to help us fight through all the obstacles.

Don't miss out!

Visit the website below and you can sign up to receive emails whenever Erica Frost publishes a new book. There's no charge and no obligation.

https://books2read.com/r/B-A-YRSV-NAIOC

BOOKS 2 READ

Connecting independent readers to independent writers.

Did you love *The Comeback*? Then you should read *Ruthless Rival*[1] by Erica Frost!

I'm a woman on the way up. My brother's best friend is the glass ceiling. In my last year at Harvard Law School, I'm in an internship at the firm of my dreams.My main competition: my brother's charming, handsome—cutthroat—best friend.I'm the only one who's onto him.Everyone else only sees how smooth and confident he is.I grew up with him and I know where that confidence comes from.He'll smile in your face and fight dirty behind your back.If he takes this job, I lose everything I've worked for.So I'll ignore his gorgeous looks and his smoking hot body, and be ready for his sleazy schemes.I've played by the rules 'til now, but for him, I'll throw the rules out.And if he thinks the way to this job is through my heart, he's in for a big

---

1. https://books2read.com/u/bPeKj7

2. https://books2read.com/u/bPeKj7

surprise.Ruthless Rival is a standalone new adult romance with a HEA and NO cheating!

Also by Erica Frost

Seduced By A Billionaire
Dark Secrets
A Billionaire's Game
Power Play
Ruthless Rival
Taming The Billionaire
The Hated Billionaire
3-Pointer
Baby For The Billionaire
My Best Friend's Brother
Ruthless Rival
The Comeback